Muchchad Gadh and Other Stories

Sangita P Menon Malhan

Vitasta
Let Knowledge Spread

Published by
Renu Kaul Verma
Vitasta Publishing Pvt Ltd
2/15, Ansari Road, Daryaganj
New Delhi-110 002
info@vitastapublishing.com

ISBN 978-93-86473-16-5

Disclaimer
All persons portrayed in this book are fictitious. Any resemblance to real persons, living or dead, is purely co-incidental.

Cover: Geetali Baruah
Printed by Vikas Computer and Printers

Dedication

For Kanwaldeep, whose friendship is among the greatest gifts of my life.

And…For
All the wonderful Oaks in my life—animate and inanimate...
For friends and well-wishers…For a superlative family…
For all the intoxicating Art in the world…
For Sculpture, Architecture, Music and Language…
For poetry and prose…For sunlight, silence and shade…
For the beauty of the hills …For the mystery of the seas…

For colours and emotions…For the strength that comes from trees…
For learning…and unlearning…For accepting and… for letting go…
For each and every blessing that has come my way…
For every benevolent gesture that has made my day…
For all the gracious people who've embellished my life…
And most of all…for 'you'...Dear reader…
A patron of the short story as a genre.
May your tribe survive!

Contents

Preface

I don't know why I write short stories. I also don't know why I don't write full-fledged novels. Somehow, the appeal of this tiny tale is never too drab for me. The brevity of the punch has remained attractive since 2009 when I suddenly found myself spinning these yarns. Pun intended! I'm thrilled when an idea overtakes me, and I'm equally relieved when it has spent itself in my arms and left me, thereby making room for another thought to walk in. All I know is that I am intoxicated by these stories that get written around me. I am sometimes aware of them, and at other times, read them later, just as you will now do. It's difficult to explain the headiness of a short but potent high. Just imagine the dead of the night. Imagine a vacuum! Imagine someone whispering something into your ears. Somewhat hallucination! Somewhat dream! Nothing very tangible. Everything crystal clear. No preconceived diegesis. An untruth! The whiff of a storyline! Someone's name. The scent of betrayal. A torn-open jugular. The softness of her lips. The fall from a thousand-foot cliff. The cackle of geese. The sound of a scythe. The constant knocking on a door. Your door. The inability to get up and answer that call. His grip on your neck. The blinding light of that sword. The sorrow of achievement. The complete desperation of need. Having to smile. Willing to die. All this and more. Anything can be provocative. Everything inspires. Such is my relationship with this genre. And I bow to its power and to its beauty. May it always be mine!

Acknowledgement

Cheers to Renu Kaul Verma at Vitasta Publishing for reacting so positively to the idea of the short story, and for bringing out this collection. And, to the artist, Bipasha Sen Gupta, for introducing me to her. I'd like to thank Veena Batra for her editorial inputs, and everyone else who has contributed to this process.

I owe my fascination for short stories to my father, the late Kenath Padmanabhan Menon, who would narrate them to me and my sister every night when we were children, growing up in Madurai. I don't think I've ever forgotten how they made me feel.

Let me also thank all the generous people who made it possible for me to have a good time while I was getting cured.

My complete gratitude to my husband, Tejinder, who stood like the Rock of Gibraltar by my side; unflinching and untired. He would blend juices of various hues whenever he was in town; they were meant to boost my blood count; and he showed me so many fantastic films. He repeatedly heard me out when I spoke of my discomfort and told me that it would all soon be over. He must have gone through his own mental anguish but he never let me know of it, bearing it silently and secretly. I wish you didn't have to go through this, Teji. All my love to You!

A warm hug and much gratitude to Dr Supriya Bali, friend and guardian angel for checking on me each and every day since all this began. She was with me every step of the way; whether it was during the time I was being re-stitched or when they were removing the chemo port from the chest. I can never forget the fact that she held my hand throughout, literally and otherwise. Thank you, Supriya. But for you, this would've been very difficult. I send you my love.

My complete and utter gratitude to my confidant of over twenty years—Kanwaldeep Singh. He not only kept a close watch over my condition—mental, emotional and physical but also made sure that I was not losing my sanity. The bitter taste in the mouth, which I continued to endure (in April 2017), nearly drove me up the wall. Each time,

I picked up the phone and told him how I was feeling, and each time, he was there to counsel me. He brought me medicines and fruits and candies. He was always there, checking to see if I was okay, and ready with a pep talk whenever I needed one. I bow to you, K! And, dedicate this collection to you!

To my brother Nishant, to my sister Sarita and to my son, Avii—You enrich my life. Spending time with the three of you is absolutely therapeutic for me. To my mum-in-law, Raminder Walia, who showed both compassion and understanding, Thank You, Mumma! My salutations to Kanwaldeep's mother, Kuljit Kaur, for being an inspiration.

This journey has brought me many gifts. Among those some absolutely gorgeous women—large-hearted and full of life. Bear hugs to Valarie Goveia, Bipasha Sen Gupta, Nikita Kansal Gupta and Rashmi Sharma Malik.

Bipasha reacted quickly when she found out about the cancer; calling up a friend of hers who had endured it and getting me to speak to her, thus helping me prepare myself for the task ahead. Nikita rushed over one evening after work with cranberries, turmeric and ginger; blended it and coaxed me to drink up the concoction. Who can forget stuff like that! She also constantly updated me on "healthy" food options.

I can also still visualize Val standing guard over me two days after my first session while I struggled with some "stomach issues" in the rest room, on her own birthday, and repeatedly wanting to know whether I was okay. Much love to you, Val. A warm embrace for Rashmi for her alternative therapy; her sea salts, her reiki, her empathy, her prayers and all her wishes. Each of these women looked out for me throughout the process and brought me great joy with their presence.

Special thanks to Soniya Mehrotra for innumerable lunches (particularly the ones after the chemo sessions) and several tea time snacks and large bottles of tomato soup; her consistent care and sincere concern. Thanks to Praveen Pramanick for a lavish Chinese feast and a pakora treat one evening; and for driving me to a radiation session once. I thank Anju Verma for her delicious soups and Suman Kumar for a wonderful dinner.

Much love to my cousin-in-law, Gigi Raikhy, for her time and empathy. Thanks are also due to Jaya Roy and Nihar Parida, who turned up one evening with a basket full of mouth-watering delicacies and some elevating conversation. Cheers to my colleagues and friends from the National Cadet Corps, who called from across the country and the world, to check on me. Salut to my pal, Sanjay Kaw, for having kept in touch with me throughout the treatment, and beyond.

Many many thanks also to the doctors in charge of my treatment—Dr Nitesh Rohatgi, Dr Harleen Nayyar and Dr Charu Garg, and to my extremely sweet nurse, Neethumol NP. She looked after me with great dedication, and smiled a lot as I practiced my Malayalam with her. That was fun!

Despicable Man

Kanakpal scratched his face as he waited for his passengers to arrive. He was the conductor of a tourist bus that plied on the roads of Uttaranchal. Today, he was scheduled to go from Ranikhet to Rishikesh, a distance of 305 kilometers. He was a native of the hilly region and had been on buses since he was sixteen. At twenty-four now, he was already a veteran; he knew the roads and the shortcuts, and he was considered an authority on the terrain. Kanakpal was also very superstitious.

His eldest brother-in-law, Sangram, was the driver of the bus; a rather laid-back, quiet man, who listened to local songs on the rickety music system, and swore very little. He smiled easily, as if he had found contentment in almost nothing and indeed everything. He was never in a hurry to get anywhere, and couldn't quite handle the fuss. It was Kanakpal, who was, therefore, in charge of operations. Or, earnings would be meagre, almost shabby.

It was mid-July and the rains had been lashing the region. It was a cruddy time to be moving on the roads. But work had to be done and tourists were aplenty. Kanakpal chewed on a beedi and waited. He was a tad jaded, having spent the last 24 hours getting the fuel tank repaired. The vehicle was anile and hoary but could run a few hundred kilometers every day even now. He called it his caravan—'a home away from home'.

It was nearly 10 am and he wanted to leave by 10.20. Within a few minutes, the passengers arrived, all at once, as if by design. There was a group of fourteen teenagers; boys and girls. They looked like they had been bitten by the city bug although they were locals. The boys wore torn jeans and flashy belts. The girls were in tight t-shirts with corny slogans on them and various shades of jeans—dark blue, indigo, black and light blue. They were mostly carrying backpacks and rucksacks and did not need to put anything in the cargo hold of the bus.

Then came a newly-wed couple; the boy was thin and swarthy but looked visibly plush with marital bliss. His shy bride had probably decided to wear western clothes for the first time. She seemed mighty uncomfortable in her loose, white baggy pants and long, shapeless red shirt. Her bangles made a clunking sound as she hauled herself into the bus, helped by her eager groom. She sat by the window, and pulled her scarf over her head. "Let it be. No one can see us now. You don't have to worry," her husband suggested. But she remained as she was. 'I must get myself a nice bride, too,' thought Kanakpal. But he wanted to marry a filmstar. Therefore, marriage had to wait for the moment.

He put away their suitcase in the furthermost corner of the baggage hold, and waited for the next lot. Sangram was still at breakfast in the roadside restaurant. He was popular with the lot there; he laughed at every crude joke, and nodded his head deferentially at the seniors. 'That man will have to be dragged out,' thought Kanakpal. 'He is so lost,' he reiterated. Sangram was indeed a day-dreamer; not the ideal driver for a tourist bus. But he was mellow and easy-going, and he followed orders without complaining. That suited Kanakpal.

This was a 42-seater bus and it had to be full before these two men could pull it out of Ranikhet. Kanakpal's prayers were soon answered. A large party of revelers, who were probably going to Rishikesh for *darshan* (a pilgrimage) turned up with too many bags and suitcases and trunks and polythene bags, and several children. The trunks had cooking utensils in them; they jingle-jangled, and created a minor racket.

The suitcases were quite heavy, and Kanakpal began shoving them into the baggage hold, without too much care. "Please be careful. There are some items of glass," said the seniormost member of this group. "Is that so? Do it yourself then, Uncle," retorted Kanakpal. That shut him up. His family hadn't heard this. Otherwise, Kanakpal might have had to pay for his tone. Such things can spark off bloody fights.

The old man sighed and said nothing. His family was getting into the bus, two by three, pushing and pulling and generally being very Indian. This meant a lot of talking and shouting; arguing over window and aisle seats; trying to accommodate more bags within the bus, under the seats in front, and being very, very shifty. But this was a group of 25 people. And that meant business. Kanakpal realized his mistake and made up by helping the old passenger into the bus, and helping him with his small polythene bags—one had oranges and the other, peanuts and biscuits and a bottle of water.

The bus was full now. Only one seat remained vacant. It was the last one at the rear end, right in the middle. "Let's go," Kanakpal called out to his brother-in-law. Meanwhile, his last passenger boarded the bus. He was an old, dirty man, dressed in rags. His coat might have been dark green, many monsoons ago. Now, it was a strange combination of black and grey and brown, covered in soot and mud. It was stinking of raw tobacco and cheap liquor.

He was unusually tall and large, and came and threw himself on that last seat. The children sitting beside him on either side withdrew, from fear and awe. He turned to look at them. Two of his lower front teeth were missing and the remaining were completely brown. Had they mustered courage, the young kids could've moved away from their spot but they remained rooted. The move seemed difficult; no picnic by far.

Their parents, who were busy chatting, hadn't noticed their consternation yet. But in a while, when they realized that the chattering had given away to complete silence, a male member turned to look back, and caught sight of this monstrous creature with his ragged looks and dirt and grime. "*Arrey bhai, suno* (Listen! Brother)," called out the man to Kanakpal. And then, he whispered in a hush, "Ask this man to move from here. He is stinking." But the man in the unsightly coat heard him and gave him a cold, menacing look. Neither Kanakpal nor the other man had the guts to say a word. They retreated.

The bus moved. It would go through Chaubattia and Najibabad, and on to Haridwar before getting to Rishikesh. Its journey would take it via the districts of Almora, Nainital, Garhwal and Tehri Garhwal, onto the

Badrinath Road. The rains had made all the roads glisten and the region looked fresh and green and breathtakingly beautiful. Some of the passengers had come to Uttaranchal for the first time.

They could not help remembering the sights in and around Ranikhet—the 'Queen's Meadow', particularly their first look at the Himalayan peak, Nanda Devi, which stood tall and majestic at 7,816 metres above sea level. They had also seen the Jhula Devi temple and the Chaubattia orchards, south of the Mall Road, and Bhaludham, an artificial lake about 3 kilometers from Ranikhet.

Their post-mortem of the trip came to a sudden halt when one of the children from the rear seat gave a whelp. He had dozed off on the dirty man's shoulder and had been awoken with a start. That had made him bang his head against the window rather violently. He had suffered a wound. "Look what you have done now," said his father, bold and courageous, for the sake of his offspring. "Couldn't you let him stay like that for a while?" he asked. The man in the ratty coat said nothing. He looked away listlessly, as if he couldn't be bothered. He immediately became unwelcome in that bus. Everyone noticed him and no one endorsed his behavior. The outcaste had become an outcaste, all over again.

He was remorseless. He had been through much worse,

and couldn't care less. No one knew that Subedar Baijnath Chand Rawat was an ex-army man; that he had an artificial leg; and that he had lost three fingers and the thumb of his right hand in a needless accident. He had also recently lost his wife to tuberculosis. He was bitter and angry and mostly suicidal after he had been removed from his job on a false molestation charge. He had lost the will to live and who knows why he was on a trip to Rishikesh.

The look on his face must have conveyed his contempt for everything and everyone around him. And when the bus halted for lunch, everyone stayed far away from him. They looked at his disfigured hand secretly as he negotiated some rotis from his coat pocket and ate them. When he bought a fresh pack of beedis from the store, they nodded their head in disapproval. "What a burden on society?" remarked one passenger.

"Why do they let such people board buses?" demanded another.

The child who had banged his head had recovered and was running around, pushing an old tyre with a stick. It rolled up to where the grungy man was seated, far away from the others, and fell at his feet. "Throw it back at the boy," said an old passenger, with a wan smile. The man in the rundown coat ignored that. He got up and made his way back to the bus. This time, he set himself down by the window. When the children got back, they did not dare ask him to move.

It had begun drizzling with a purpose, and the window shutters were being pulled together fiercely. But raindrops lashed at them with sharp intent. The bus moved slowly. It had to be even more careful now. "Do you think this is a great downpour or will it pass?" asked a passenger, of Kanakpal. The conductor looked at the horizon, and at the heavy, grey clouds at a distance. He did not have the heart to share the truth. It was going to be a deluge! They were still far from their destination, and would most definitely be late. They might even have to take a break if the rains did not relent. "It's too early to tell but we'll see," Kanakpal lied.

In time, it dawned upon some passengers that this was going to be a ride that they would not forget easily. The newly-weds huddled up closer; the groom tried to comfort his bride, and looked even more distressed than she did. The group of teenagers was unconcerned. The boys sang popular songs from Hindi films and the girls joined in. With the rain pouring about them, they had decided to restrict their songs to those about the monsoon. It was the romance, the mood. Some of the more adventurous boys looked amorously at the girls, conveying their inglorious intentions with their eyes.

The first strike of thunder rattled the bus and its travellers. And then, a huge bolt of lightning fell. It was visible from a great distance—must have been down in the hills somewhere—far, far away, but Kanakpal asked Sangram to stop the bus and park it by the side of the hilly road. You do remember me telling you that he was superstitious? "We are not moving on," he announced. There was obvious discontent among the passengers.

"Is it that serious? Other buses are plying," remarked a young boy from the loud group of crooners.

"Others might take a risk if they want to but I will not," said Kanakpal. He was adamant. He had heard from his seniors that when you saw lightning strike ahead of you, it was with a reason, with a purpose. "The time has come for someone in this bus. That lightning was meant to strike us," he declared. The passengers reacted almost unanimously; they held their breath.

"What do you mean? This is all humbug," shouted a teen. "It isn't even close to where we are," he stressed.

The rain was noisy and wild and it was difficult to hear clearly over the ruckus it was creating. Trees swayed about like angry, unruly elephants and lashed their branches at everything coming in their way. "If this sort of thing is true, we must then find out who it is meant for," suggested a young girl from the group. Some passengers turned to look at the man in the dirty, old coat. He looked like a candidate who fitted the bill.

"But we can't keep standing by the road. We must move to a safer area," suggested a passenger. He had already accosted Kanakpal and had begun advising him. The bus remained where it was.

"I am not moving an inch," Kanakpal insisted.

"But we'll get really late," complained the passengers.

They had got up and were standing in the aisle, jostling one another, for no apparent reason. Someone lost his balance, and several people tumbled, one after the other; the last man standing fell with a huge thud on the passenger with the dirty coat. The `Despicable Man' (he had been named so by some ingenious youngster) was probably dozing. He got with a start and gave the fat man who fell on him a resounding slap.

His fellow travellers were shocked. "Someone should get this one off the bus," one whispered.

"Let me tell you what we'll do," Kanakpal announced. "I'm sure that death awaits one of us. A lightning strike just a few kilometers from us is a sure sign of that," he proclaimed. No one knew any better. So, they did not protest. "Each one of us will get down from the bus, and go and touch that elm tree, yonder. I'm not going to sacrifice all of us for that one unfortunate person," he said.

A shiver went down every spine in that blessed vehicle. "But this is ridiculous. It is pouring so heavily. We'll be soaked to our skin. Besides, what if the lightning catches me," asked a passenger.

"Then, the rest of us will just move on," joked his friend, and was ribbed in the chest. Sangram spoke for the first time that day. "Please hurry. This is not safe at all. I cannot stay parked here forever," he implored.

The group of teenagers was the first to volunteer. A boy borrowed a raincoat from Kanakpal and got down from the bus, a little hesitantly. He ran to the large tree. Kanakpal was urging him to go right up to it and touch it. It was obvious that he was petrified. He just stood there, cowering in the rainstorm and not moving an inch. Kanakpal grabbed his umbrella and rushed to the boy. "Just touch it and go back to the bus," he shouted at the boy.

Shaken by the urgency in that voice, the boy put his hand out and touched the tree. The other passengers watched anxiously from the bus. Nothing transpired. The boy was safe. Jolted back to shape by his good fortune, he began running back to the vehicle. Cars went by in the ferocious rain, and some motorcycles, too, but no bus had overtaken theirs yet. When he finally managed to get in, the boy recovered some of his colour. His friends picked up resolve too, and one by one, they went up to the tree, and touched it. They were all unscathed. Nothing untoward happened.

The groom was trying to convince his wife to let him go. She had begun crying hopelessly. "Please don't go," she begged of him. "Why don't you stay with her a little longer? I'll ask my family members to go first," offered the old man, who seemed to be the seniormost in the group of 25 people. "Perhaps we should also follow the routine so that we can be done with it quickly and then move on," he suggested. His family remained rooted to its spot. No one wanted to be the first to go.

'Death must be waiting for me,' thought the old man to himself. "I'll go," he said. Still, no one came forward. They were perhaps hoping that he would be proven right. No one wanted to die just yet. They were relatively young. "C'mon! C'mon! We don't have all day here," prodded Kanakpal. The old man took one step very gingerly out of the bus. The rain caught him in his jaw and whizzed past his shroud. The ground was slippery. He walked very, very slowly, with a stick in one hand. Thunder rumbled. Some passengers jumped from their seats.

It was taking very long for the old man to reach the tree. He touched it. There was a loud crackling sound but nothing spectacular happened. The old man returned to the bus. His family members showed respite for him but were frightened for themselves now. Twenty-four people went through the routine, each one losing a little blood on the face, and many, missing heartbeats. Something divine was protecting them, they reckoned.

The big guy in the dirty coat lit up a *beedi* in the bus, and the fumes went up to the passengers. They complained loudly, this time. "Put it out," said one. He did not pay heed. He was seated rather comfortably on the back seat because the children had abandoned it to huddle up to their parents. The lapels of his coat had fallen to one side, showing a hunter's knife, tucked into a belt. He put his dismembered hand on the knife. There wasn't a second appeal or order for the *beedi* to be extinguished.

"Send this one. He must be the person death is looking for," said the man, in a rebound.

"Looks like a small-time crook to me," replied his friend. "More like a thug," pointed out another.

There was some drama in the bus as the bride clung to her husband as he got up to fulfill his part of the responsibility. No one questioned Kanakpal's superstitious assumptions. They presumed that such things were true of the mysterious hills. It was dark by now, and one could not see the tree very clearly. "Let me come with you. We'll die together, if we have to," she beseeched. Dramatic!

Her husband was impressed. "We'll go together," he

announced and put the raincoat on her. He himself took refuge under a large multi-coloured umbrella, which was on its last legs. They looked quite pitiable, walking out like that. The bride was still crying. Her *kaajal* had smudged her cheeks and her red *bindi* was all over her forehead. She was holding on to a locket with a picture of a God with one hand, and with the other, she clutched on to her husband.

There was enough slush, and as he dragged her along, she slipped and fell and cut her ankle on a stone. Her Gods were sending her signs; she was sure that they were going to die. Her white trouser got a bit of the blood; he was shaking like a leaf. They touched the tree, and waited for death. Nothing happened. Relieved, and taken aback by this stroke of luck, they scampered back to the bus, like uncaring children. She was limping a bit but quite relieved that they had been saved. Fellow passengers welcomed her back on board. One said, "See, it was easy." The girl looked at him; she was pale and grimacing with pain. She had also twisted her foot.

The passengers now turned to look at the man in the scummy coat. They were all safe. He would be the last one to go. "C'mon! It is your turn," said Kanakpal. The Despicable Man did not react. He spoke with a slur. "I don't believe in this baloney. I've been watching this circus for so long. Now that you've all had a chance, just move on," he ordered. He had a commanding voice.

"But...but... all of us went up to the tree. You have to do it, too. Otherwise, I'm not going on," muttered Kanakpal with very little force in his voice. He was begging this man to move.

"I don't care what you think. I'm not getting out in this torrid rain. This is the only coat I have," he said. It seemed like a losing battle of wits. The passengers looked at one another; their eyes mirroring their anxiety and their lack of pluck. They knew that no one could take on this man. He seemed too strong for them, and he had a knife. Then, a genial, elderly man got up from his seat, which was right ahead, and wormed his way to the back.

"My son," he began. "Please do this so that the bus can move. We need to get out of this zone. It is dangerous, and we have been parked here for nearly two hours," he said in a soft voice. "Besides, do you want to be blamed for everyone else's misery?" he asked. God only knows what happened when the old man said, 'Blamed'. The Despicable Man moved. He pushed aside the raincoat that he was being offered, and the umbrella; pulled his coat closer to his body, and got out of the bus. "Death, here I come!" he announced.

Everyone was relieved. They were also curious about what they were about to witness. The man in the dirty coat stood by the bus for a while, not moving. He looked here and there. Forty-three pairs of eyes rested on his frame. He began trudging towards the tree, at his own unhurried pace. His coat was soaked already, and the wind tried to tear it off his person. But he was stoic. He moved on languidly. He was a few inches from the tree when he turned to look at the bus. He was about to put his hand on the tree when lightning struck the vehicle. It went up in flames!

****

The Irrepressible Mr Phull

Phul Saab and Phull Saab were not colleagues. But they ended up spending a lot of time together. It was a quirk of fate. Mr Phul was an engineer with the South-Eastern Railway. A reticent, sober man, he worked hard and spent his free time with his family which consisted of his wife, Kiranjit, and their sons, Ravi and Shashi.

The other Mr Phull was a gregarious consultant with an engineering company called Mecon. His wife Gurmeet was equally noisy, and his teenaged sons, Mohinder and Rupinder, incorrigible. A cacophonous lot, they were repeatedly ticked off at school. Prithpal Singh Phul and Jagmandir Singh Phull first met in Ranchi when they were both posted there. The former did not use the surname Phul but Jagmandir found out about it and instantly struck up a blood relation.

Jagmandir was a friend of Prithpal's brother-in-law who worked in the construction sector, and who also participated in the functioning of the local gurdwara. There had been some stories about Jagmandir having had some mishaps at work, but other than that, he was supposed to be a fine fellow—a bit rough around the edges but very helpful and simple.

Soon after they were introduced, Jagmandir declared that Prithpal was a 'good friend'. He sat with him during the prayers in the gurdwara, talking incessantly and making Prithpal very uncomfortable. When the prayers were over, he began walking with Prithpal. "Come! Let's go home and have a nice cup of tea," he offered. Who knew that he was self-inviting himself to Prithpal's home!

The children started playing cricket in the front yard. Gurmeet joined Kiranjit in the kitchen. She began talking about her in-laws, criticizing them, of course. Kiranjit realized that this was going to be a long, tiring afternoon. Both Phulls were very talkative. There were neither commas nor colons in their monologues. And, they always overstayed their welcome. This continued for six months. The Phulls went over to Prithpal's place nearly every evening!

Therefore, it was an enormous relief when Prithpal announced to his family one night that he had been transferred to Jagdalpur, a sleepy town in the Bastar region of central India. Prithpal was going to do a project to enable electric trains to ply there. The children would have to go to a boarding school in Mussoorie and Kiranjit would temporarily shift to her parents' home in Ludhiana. She would take up a job there, teaching English literature to post-graduate students. The family had seen the last of the Phulls. Everyone was thrilled.

Prithpal's work took him to remote areas in Orissa, Bihar, Andhra Pradesh and Madhya Pradesh. Ravi and Shashi were told stories of Baila Dila and Kirandul in Orissa. There were tales from the hill town of Koraput, and from Jharsagoda. Their father had also worked at Khurda and Khurda Road. These last two places were notorious for their bandit attacks and burglaries. The children heard these stories with rapt attention.

In Madhya Pradesh, Prithpal and his team set up the equipment for trains to ply in Dalli Raja Ra and Katni. In Andhra Pradesh, work was done near Arku. Much groundwork also went into Chakradharpur—a municipality in the west Singhbhum district, now in Jharkhand. Located in the Chotanagpur Plateau, it lies 62 kilometres west of Jamshedpur. Finally, there was Jagdalpur, right in the heart of what would later become Chattisgarh—a tribal belt with its mysterious adivasis, "who walked about naked and carried bows and arrows tipped with poison". At least, that's what the kids were told!

When the summer vacations drew near, Prithpal's family congregated in Jagdalpur. The children were then taken to the Chitrakoot falls, the broadest waterfalls in India, and to the Dandakaranya Forests (Jungles of Punishment). Characters from the Indian epic, Ramayana, are believed to have roamed here during their exile.

The children also spent time near the railway tracks; loitered about the yard and climbed onto stationary engines. Hardly four or five trains passed by each day. Therefore, the catchment area was safe. There was another 'railway family' nearby. This couple from south India, Srividya and Srinivas Reddy, had two children—a boy called Daryao, who was thirteen, and a girl of nine, Samyogita.

They became a gang. Ravi and Daryao hit it off, and Samyogita and Shashi were a team. The older children were both extroverts; out-going, active and innovative. They often went to a shop called the 'Dancing Cactus' that sold wood art. Daryao was an amateur artisan. He'd pick up pieces of wood, discarded by the shop owners for want of perfection, and carve them with remarkable skill.

The kids also watched trains as they went past on the metre gauge. They were particularly fascinated with the 'hoop wheel' ceremony. When a train passed by, the driver tossed out a wheel made of bamboo. A station worker stood on a narrow black slab by the tracks and caught it. He would then exchange a hoop, and the driver was supposed to catch it. "If the hoop isn't caught, the trains cannot move any further," Daryao told the other kids. They believed him.

The children were also particularly fond of a little red train, which they had named the 'Jiggling Jyotilakshmi'. It was tiny, and it moved with a rhythmic, musical spurt, like a dancer. It was so slow that they could get on and off it with absolute ease. They even competed with each other to see who could do it the fastest. 'Jyotilakshmi' sometimes stood in the yard, and the children sat by the engine, and ate chironjee, a dry fruit native to that area.

One July morning, as the children played, they saw some familiar faces in the distance. It had to be a hallucination. Jagmandir Singh Phull had pursued their father and landed up in Jagdalpur. Ravi and Shashi ran home to warn their mother. "Believe it or not, Ma, Mr Phull is here. And, he's headed for our place. Should we warn Papa?" Before she could brace herself, there they were—all four of them, walking into the house, and greeting her with much gusto.

Kiranjit looked for their luggage. They didn't have any. She thanked God for small mercies. At least they weren't going to stay with them. "Hello, Mrs Phul! Isn't this wonderful? How are you? And, how is my favourite pal?" asked Mr Phull. Kiranjit gave Jagmandir her best fake smile and said, "What a surprise! Welcome! Welcome! He'll be out in a minute. He's just writing some letters. Let me inform him."

Phull Saab hugged his 'namesake' with ferocity. He was a large, rugged man, with hairy arms. Prithpal managed to extricate himself from the embrace. He looked desolate at the intrusion and knew that his day was ruined. Had the man been posted here, as well, he wondered. Jagmandir, on the other hand, was overjoyed to see his friend. They had been apart for nearly a year.

He explained the nature of his visit. His seniors had insisted that he take up an assignment in Jagdalpur, and he couldn't refuse. He was going to be there for about two months. He then began advising Prithpal on how the railways ought to handle its project in the region. There was to be no let-up even during lunch. The man could talk!

At 6.30 pm, there was still no sign that Phull Saab would leave. In fact, he had sent word for some other acquaintances of theirs to join in the fun. Lankesh Mishra and Sivamohan Rao, two engineers with a great sense of humour and many redoubtable anecdotes, turned up. Drinks were brought out and so were the snacks. Kiranjit's feet were killing her and she had a splitting headache. At 7.30 pm, these men got up to leave. Lankesh couldn't be the raconteur that he usually was. Jagmandir had interrupted him throughout the evening, and preempted his jokes.

Prithpal hoped that Jagmandir would get up, too, but he showed no signs of exhaustion. In fact, he was trying to convince the others to hang on for dinner. "Do stay! You must absolutely try Kiranjit's Murg Pulao and Badaami Tangri. I can still remember the flavor of those dishes. And, how could I ever forget that pink coconut burfi," he said with sincerity. His fingers went up to his mouth to show appreciation.

Lankesh seemed tempted. But no invite had been forthcoming from Kiranjit. She smiled apologetically. She hadn't even cooked these things for the night. It was going to be simple fare—dal, rice, vegetables and rotis. And, some Benarasi kheer. "Yes, of course. Do have dinner with us, although I've haven't had time to marinate the chicken," she said. Lankesh was a smart chap. He took the cue, and decided to go home. Sivamohan said something about his wife having made her signature sambar for dinner. He had to leave, as well. But Jagmandir was here for the night. He wasn't budging.

Prithpal's spirits sank. He had spent almost eight hours with this man, and could not last one more minute. He went out to the porch to see off his guests. "He's quite a handful, isn't he?" ribbed Siva. "I have strict orders from the missus to warn her before this one comes home. She still hasn't got over his last visit." He laughed.

"Where was this?" asked Prithpal. "In Ranchi?" Siva nodded. "He just turned up one Sunday morning, and left only at midnight. He also complained about the excessive spice and tamarind in her food, and that didn't go down well with her," he chuckled. "Get him to leave now. Or, you may have to hear him go on and on for the next four hours," he pointed out, before leaving. Prithpal sighed. It was the hapless sigh of the courteous host. He didn't have it in him to be unrefined and direct. He was a gentleman, and he had a great deal of patience. "I wish someone would take him away, for me," he thought before getting back into the house.

He went straight to the kitchen to see if his wife was alright. Dinner had to be made, and he knew that she didn't like to cook such a lot. There was absolutely no sound from the living room. Mr Phull may have gone to the men's room. "I'm so sorry about this, my dear. What can I do?" Prithpal asked his wife.

"Don't worry. We'll manage," she assured him. "Go! Check on Mr Phull," she nudged. Gurmeet had gone to her quarter to take a phone call from her mother. The children were still playing outside.

Prithpal returned to the living room. He couldn't believe his eyes. All four cushions in the room were under Jagminder's body. One under his head, two under his legs and one under his arm. The irrepressible Mr Phull had crashed out on the sofa. He was snoring. The children came in, and began staring at him, as well. They had never seen him so still. Gurmeet returned.

"Listen! My mother was saying that you forgot to leave the spare key to the house with her. How will she get it cleaned before Mamaji arrives? You can be so forgetful," she began. Kiranjit put her forefinger to her lips, motioning her to be quieter. She then took her to Mr Phull. Gurmeet cocked her head to one side, and moved it, not at all surprised.

"So, he dozed off," was her reaction. Kiranjit raised her eyebrows. "He suffers from hypersomnia, you see," explained Gurmeet. "He falls asleep suddenly, sometimes at work, and often when he's reading. Once, he fell asleep at the wheel. My God! That was scary! Anything could've happened. But he told me that his system just shut down. That is why, I think, he tries to remain so active; never ceasing to talk and always so restless." She smiled at her hosts, a little embarrassed but resilient. Kiranjit switched off the ceiling lights in the living room, put her arm around Gurmeet's shoulder, and they walked away towards the kitchen.

It was time for a nice cup of ginger tea, and then, dinner!

****

Game in Gorakhpur

nspector Hanumanth Kewat was on his rounds of the city. He had been posted at the old police station, the Kotwali Thana in Maya Bazar in north Gorakhpur for four years now as the Station Officer. His khakhi uniform was well-ironed, and his rank insignia shone under the morning sun—three silver stars on a red and blue striped ribbon at the outer edge of the shoulder strap. He was feeling quite bright and energetic; an athletic-looking man, who was large without being bulky, and who was known for his agility and shrewdness.

The inspector moved through the congested Maya Bazar which was teeming with morning workers. Some were biting into bits of Imarti, a local delicacy, orange in colour and dripping with sugar. Yet others were munching the Baati Chokha with its potato and egg plant mix. Tempos, tongas, autos and rickshaws jostled for space with motorbikes, scooters and cycles. The place was swamped with four wheelers too. For the sake of mobility and easy access through that sort of congestion, the inspector always opted for his motorbike over his official jeep.

Moving past Kasia Road, also called the Doctor's Road (several renowned physicians practised here), he went past the Bhalotia market, which was the largest market for drugs (medicines) in the city. He then turned towards Golghar and the Town Hall. Something caught his eye and he brought his vehicle to a screeching halt as he tried to make out the appearance of the man he saw from some distance at a crossing. It just could not be! It had to be an illusion!

But there was little mistaking that pronounced cleft in the jaw, the bushy eyebrows, and that long, savage hair. The man who had suddenly come into Inspector Kewat's line of sight was buying a cigarette from a shop across the road. He must have sensed someone's eyes on him because he looked left and right, and then, he met the inspector's gaze. Alarm rested on his brow for just a fleeting second. Then, he hopped on his motorbike and began riding away.

The inspector kicked his machine into action and began pursuing the apparition. His mind was in a tizzy. This was simply not possible. He remembered quite clearly that he had himself hunted down and finally arrested this man after a long and tiresome pursuit of eight-and-a-half years. Jibbal Sainthwar was the most notorious petty thief, thug and looter in all Gorakhpur district.

The police had been at his heels for over a decade and he had evaded them each time. Jibbal had over 150 counts of various charges filed against him, from minor break-ins to burglaries to instigating agrarian riots to petty cattle thefts to the occasional murder. He did not indulge in chain-snatching though; it was far too commonplace for a seasoned lawbreaker like him.

Jibbal's ancestors had kept company with the descendants of the Badhaks, the Doms and the armed gangs of dacoits beyond the Nepal border, and had been extremely well-networked. And he, too, had sympathetic elements protecting him; some, even in the police force, it was feared.

For Inspector Kewat, it had become his life's mission to track Jibbal down and put him behind bars. He had done that, last year. So, how could Jibbal be out and roaming freely? For a moment, the inspector thought of calling the Kotwali and asking his staff to check on Jibbal's whereabouts. But then, the man was on the run and needed to be deftly pursued.

Jibbal's bike skilfully manoeuvred the crammed roads,

going past the District Court and then turning towards the Bus Stand area. Inspector Kewat was hot on his heels. The man kept turning to look at his pursuer. The bikes went past the Hanuman Temple in the south, and then headed for the Imambara Degree College on the west side. They were covering the entire parameter of the city.

Much as he tried, Inspector Kewat could not close the gap with his prey. Jibbal's bike aimed for the road that would eventually lead him to the National Highway 28. It then picked up great speed and vanished from sight. Inspector Kewat stopped and cursed liberally in Bhojpuri.

When he entered the Kotwali, the back of his shirt was soaked with sweat. He was furious and seemed completely out-of-sorts. He called out for a change of shirt, and when a constable brought it to him, he asked for his second-in-command to be sent to his office.

Sub Inspector Babban Pipraich was a smooth talker, thick-skinned and corrupt. He was suspected of having let several criminal offenders grease his palm. He was also well-connected with the hoi-polloi. His elder sister's husband worked at the Police Headquarters in Lucknow. So, he feared no or little backlash. He had clout.

If Inspector Kewat knew about Babban's dark side, he did not show it on that day. He had questions of his own and he wanted answers. Moreover, he took the Uttar

Pradesh Police motto—'The Protection of the Good and the Destruction of the Bad'—very seriously. He had an untarnished reputation and had never been pulled up for dereliction of duty. It was widely known that he was incorruptible. He did not suffer from any vices and he had no ailments.

"Babban, what is the update on Jibbal Sainthwar? Wasn't he holed up in Azamgarh district? Or was it Ballia?" Kewat asked.

"From what I remember, Sir, he was first taken to Jaunpur and then to Chandauli, where he continued to create trouble. So, he was moved to Maharajganj. But I can check and report to you," Babban replied.

"Do it at once," the Station House Officer ordered. He sat at his desk trying to ensure that it was indeed Jibbal Sainthwar whom he had pursued all morning. Copies of some local newspapers including *Amar Ujala, Dainik Jagran*, *Aaj* and *Swatantra Chetna* were lying about. He picked up one listlessly; his attention lay elsewhere.

Babban made a few calls, and returned to say, "Sir, he is very much in Maharajganj. They say that he might remain there for very long." The inspector was eminently foxed but sent the sub-inspector away. He needed to think hard. What if he had been wrong? After all, he had seen the man for but only a minute. He had not got a good close look at him. People do make mistakes. But if the man was not Jibbal, why did he flee? And the hair and its orange-brown colour was quite distinct.

The inspector called for tea and stepped out of his office. The day had been uneventful so far barring a truck collapse near the Public Works Department zonal office in east Gorakhpur, which had caused a whopping traffic snarl. Kattas had been drawn out during the brawl, and the police had to step in to contain everyone involved. Save that, there was nothing of consequence, yet.

The major crimes would be reported during the day, and many of them, the next morning. As he put his cup down, an envelope was brought up to the inspector's office. He tore it open. Inside it was a piece of paper. It said, "Gave you the slip again. Watch your back! *Hum naahin bhulali.* (I haven't forgotten!)" Quite audacious!

The officer went to the courtyard behind the thana. Rage surged within him like a tearing storm. How dare the miscreant mock him! There was no doubt now that Jibbal Sainthwar had broken out of prison. Should he sound an alert? Should he call Maharajganj himself and double-check the information that Babban had given him?

He decided to visit the place. He called up his superior and confided in him. "But are you certain?" he was asked. Kewat told him about the letter.

"This is highly irregular. But carry on," said the senior. Police stations are fiercely possessive about jurisdictions, and the visit was to be managed wisely. Luckily for him, Kewat knew the Station House Officer posted there.

Maharajganj was about 55 kilometres away; it would take about an hour and a half to get there. Getting off the jeep, as Kewat walked into the station, he wondered what would happen. It was *Mulakat* hour, when families of prisoners were able to visit them. "How's Jibbal doing?" Kewat asked his colleague, Ulagan Turaiha, without revealing anything yet.

"Oh! That rogue? He's a bit of a pain but we know how to break him," said Turaiha, scratching his belly; he had put on a lot of weight.

Kewat's heart sank. So, Jibbal was here, after all. How could the inspector have been so mistaken? Was someone playing a dangerous game? Why did he lead himself to believe that his suspicion held water? The whole episode was going to be painfully embarrassing.

Turaiha intervened. "His uncle is visiting him right now. Do you want to see him? What is this about?" he probed.

"We have to verify something about his arrest. I believe his gang is active again," replied Kewat. The entire region knew of Kewat's conquest. His visit wasn't seen as unusual.

"Very well, then. Please carry on," said Turaiha. His team had just raided a notorious gang of bootleggers in Maharajganj, and there was enough paper work to be done.

Kewat walked to the small Interview Hall which had a see-through glass wall. His head was reeling. Some microphones had been installed for visitors to be able to communicate with their relatives who were languishing behind those partitions. And then, Jibbal's face came into view. There's no two ways about the fact that it was indeed 'he'. In fact, the thug was looking better than before; the cleft in his jaw was less pronounced because he had put on some meat on his face and he looked cleaner. Prison life was suiting him.

Facing him was an elderly man in a disheveled light brown kurta pyjama. The men were speaking softly until Jibbal saw his nemesis; the man who had brought all his unholy endeavours to a complete halt. "Inspector Sahib! *Kaisan baa?* (How are you?) To what do we owe this honour?" he asked unabashedly. Jibbal's uncle got up deferentially. "Please sit, Janaab," he offered. "I am about to leave, in any case," he pointed out. He looked like a pious man, who seemed to be completely out of place in the slammer.

"Okay, son. Look after yourself. And let us pray that justice will come to you," he added softly. He brought his hands up to his chest to greet the inspector. A picture of Lord Bhairav was engraved on the corrugated skin of his right wrist, just barely visible beneath the long sleeve of the kurta, with his name, Vajradhar, written below that. Jibbal had the same tattoo, with his name written under the mark. Was this a family tradition or was it a mark of the Sainthwar gang of thieves?

When the old man left, Kewat got to the point. He joined Jibbal inside the Interview Hall. "Why did you send me that letter? What game are you playing?" he asked angrily.

Jibbal gave him a sly smile. "Inspector Sahib. What are you talking about? This prison is my humble abode now. I have been incarcerated here for life. You are not making much sense," he said, wryly. He did not look flustered nor did he shift in his seat. His confidence angered Inspector Kewat even more.

"You and I both know that you were in Gorakhpur the other day. C'mon. Out with it! What's the plan?" Kewat pushed forth. He held Jibbal by the scruff of his shirt collar, and gave him a hard tug. The prisoner stayed calm. "No games, Jibbal, I warn you. No tricks, or I will see to it that you are unable to move even one tiny muscle in that body," threatened the inspector.

Jibbal did not attempt to free himself but he looked

Kewat straight in the eye and said, "Listen to yourself talk, Inspector. I have been in prison for a year now. I have never been out of the precinct. I have no idea what you mean. And you know that you've made a huge mistake." Kewat pushed the man away in disgust and stormed out of the hall warning, "I'll be watching you, Jibbal. I'll be watching you." Jibbal walked indifferently away from the Interview Hall, with not a care in the world. He was a hardened offender, and such threats did not ruffle him in the least.

But the events of the last few days took their toll on Inspector Kewat. He managed to save face with his superior although he was given a 'talk'. And then, the worst happened. The inspector saw Jibbal again in the city, two weeks thereafter. The pattern was more or less similar. He was on his bike, on a round, and he saw Jibbal racing ahead of him. He followed him all over again, and lost him, once more. But this time, he made no mention of the incident whatsoever. Perhaps, he was seeing things.

Inspector Kewat was but a social drinker but now he wished he were an alcoholic; that kindred spirit would have helped numb his senses and drown out some of the confusion. "But I know that I am right. How can I be wrong?" he asked himself, over and over again. He kept his eyes open for many weeks after that, hoping to catch sight of Jibbal on the city's roads, someday. But nothing of the sort happened. It was as if Jibbal would never return to haunt Hanumanth Kewat ... until four months later.

A late night sojourn had kept the inspector on the streets until 2 am. He was tired and hungry and sleepy, and he had had a long ride cutting through Gangotri Vihar colony with its tight alleys. He had also visited the SSP Residence area and the DDU Gorakhpur University precincts. It was rumoured that trouble was brewing in some of these parts. Visits had also been made to the District Magistrate's Residence and to the MP Inter College areas before winding up at the Charuchandrapuri Colony in the south-east of the city. When he finally returned to the Kotwali police station, it was already 3 am. Another letter was waiting for him. It asked, "Are you rattled?"

Seething with rage, the inspector picked up his jeep, and decided to rush to Maharajganj at once. "But it is late, Sahib. Is it an emergency?" asked a constable, gingerly. Inspector Kewat said nothing. Two constables tried to accompany him. He discouraged them. He was going to do this alone. Thirty kilometers into the journey, he was still fuming inexorably. 'I must ensure that Jibbal is in prison at this very moment,' he told himself. He was lost in thought and did not see two trucks closing in on him. One overtook him and the other pinned him from the rear. His jeep had to halt.

It was dark and eerily quiet. No one moved from the trucks. Experience had taught Kewat that such silence was potent and that it could be lethal. He moved slowly towards the driver's seat of the truck that was ahead of his vehicle, trying to stay alert and sharp. But the ambush happened so quickly that even he could not thwart it. Someone leapt at him with full force and threw him off balance. He went sprawling on the road, and reached for the gun in his holster.

But Jibbal's hands were quicker. He brought out his knife and in one clean sweep, sent it swishing past the inspector's jugular vein. Blood began sprouting off his neck. It was a perfect cut. Holding on to his neck, the inspector looked up, shocked, into Jibbal's unforgiving eyes. "Didn't I warn you that I would avenge myself?" the man sneered. He then dragged the inspector away from the road into the dark bushes.

Kewat's head spun with questions. If this was Jibbal, who was the man he had met at the Maharajganj prison? Jibbal smirked. "You're wondering what happened? Believe it or not, Inspector Sahib. You never caught me!" he said, pushing his hair away from his face. The tattoo on his hand was visible. But the name was different. It said—Bhairon.

Hanumanth Kewat stared at his killer, without comprehending. His eyes were wide open but his heart was pumping away frantically. His limbs were going numb. He was going to die. "You never arrested me," Jibbal gritted. "The man in prison is my doppelganger." With the remaining strength in his arms, the inspector tugged at 'Jibbal's' collar. The thug pushed him away, and watched coldly… as Kewat's life went out of him.

****

The Cabinet Committee Meeting

An urgent circular had been issued at 7 pm on Saturday for an emergency meeting of 'the committee' that was to be held the following morning. A serious issue needed immediate attention and would all committee members make it possible to attend the meeting! Everyone was required to put their signature on the circular. Sunday morning would have to be "sacrificed". There would be no escape.

Come Sunday, there was hectic activity in the drab 15 by 20 feet meeting room of the welfare association. It was mid-November. In forty minutes, there would be 12 people in that room; most of them senior citizens. Charlie D'Souza, the supervisor of the colony was busy giving orders and asking the guards and peons to go scurrying about. He was an emaciated, bespectacled, diffident man in his late forties, who was quite relieved when he found work in this colony. After all, who takes on a middle-aged man with not too many qualifications!

"Jagdish, get that corner cleaned, will you? And, please ask Bhurey to use a fresh swipe. Don't use the old one. It'll stink," he told one of the peons. "When you've done that, get all these files in order. You never know what they may ask for. And where is the key to the master cupboard? The minutes of the last meeting are in there. Do you have a spare pen? This one has stopped working. Where are the reports on the thefts that took place three months ago? Is there an update? And the pictures of all the trees that need pruning… where are they? Did Billimoria Sahib submit his statement of accounts?" D' Souza asked. There was too much to do.

"And where is Ravi? He has to be here," D'Souza stressed. Ravi was the de facto caretaker of the large colony. He knew everything and everyone. He was well-connected, and he had a smooth tongue, which went over bumps and roadblocks with great finesse. Association representatives approached him for all kinds of things. He could get them application forms; he could get bills paid way past their due date; he knew the local municipal councillor and could get an appointment and he knew the local beat constables by their names. And, when someone had a mishap, it was Ravi, the guard, who was contacted on his cell phone.

One could safely say that D' Souza, who had started work in this colony only last year was, in fact, serving his apprenticeship under Ravi's tutelage. By and by, it was 11 am. The meeting was scheduled to begin. The first people to arrive were ex army and air force guys; punctual and purposeful. Col (retired) Tungabhadra Aggarwal had been a doctor in the army. He walked with a limp and always dressed immaculately. He could hold his tongue and spoke only when spoken to.

Wg Cdr (also retired) RS Khanna, a large, fair man with a bald pate and large, bulbous eyes had also walked in. "How are things, Colonel? How're the ol' bones holding up?" he enquired.

"Not too bad, old boy. The cold's beginning to bother me this winter though," acknowledged the Colonel. They were soon joined by the female members of the group.

Mrs Changkija and Mrs Shah had been chosen to represent their particular blocks in the association for the second consecutive year. And, Mrs Gorain had been a part of the committee ten years ago in her previous stint. They had a lot to share. They began with the gossip. "So, did they finally get those two sisters out?" asked Mrs Gorain.

"No. They wouldn't go so easy. The police had to be

involved. And, just as the girls were about to leave their landlord walked in to support them," said Mrs Shah.

The "girls" in question had sub-let one of the servants' quarters in the colony and were rumored to be of dubious reputation. Mrs Changkija responded with just her eyes and the movement of her eyebrows. The other women acknowledged that and continued with their tales. Yet other association members sauntered in. Aparajita Lamba, a software professional, had just joined the committee and came to the meeting, curious and skeptical. She had been brought into this melee by her very social neighbor, Vipasha Seth, who was in charge of "greening" the colony.

The agenda of the day was serious. The Secretary of the Association had been absent from work for over six months. After the elections to the core committee, and once he had been selected, he had just stopped coming to office. He hadn't explained why and he did not offer a valid excuse either. With the workload increasing, the association had been exploiting the services of its previous secretary, who hereafter did not wish to have anything to do with the day-to-day running of the colony.

The absentee secretary, a real estate agent, had been accosted a few times on his way out of the colony at 11 in the morning and on his return at 10.30 pm. His response had been—"I have too much backlog at work." He just didn't have the time! He added that he had also suffered from jaundice, typhoid and measles, over the past few months. Conjunctivitis and viral fever were also in the air. Some members suspected that he was lying. Others didn't voice their opinion. There was some confusion about the sequence of his maladies, though. Did he get jaundice first? Or, was it typhoid? The reports were conflicting.

Finally, there was the announcement that his wife was pregnant after eleven years of marriage. So, could he not relinquish his post and let someone else take over? The man wasn't forthcoming with his reply on that either. The association had earlier sent him a letter asking him to make his intentions clear but his wife had not "received" it. It then went to his office, where it had been received. But his office guard confided that he had been admonished adequately for the "lapse". So, there the issue of what to do with the secretary…remained hanging in the balance.

"He won't go easy," said Vipasha. "We'll have to chuck him out," she stressed. Aparajita nodded indifferently. Mrs Shah gave her an enquiring look.

She called D' Souza. "What happened? Where is Dr Shalya? What about Shlipi? Is she expected? It is already 11.25," she noted. Just then the president walked in. Dr B D Shalya went to the head of the table, and pulling a chair, sat down.

He was a tall, strapping man of about 60 who wore a lot of jewellery. They included a gold chain with several lockets, three gold rings on each hand and a heavy gold bracelet with nine gems ensconced in it. He had been a theatre actor, and still worked on stage, sparingly. He was voluble and confident and suffered from many bad hair days. "Hello! Hello! How are you?" he asked around, and then looked at the door.

"Where's Perzan? He was walking behind me," he said. Perzan Billimoria was the treasurer of the association; a quiet, sober man in his mid-thirties. He was semi-organized; he knew his numbers well and he did not accept nonsense easily. If there was ever any confusion about the cheques received or sent out, the credit for that mess had to be squarely laid on others in that group. Billimoria thought about last year's budget and was more focused on getting that sorted out.

"Perzan, Is Mrs Soi coming?" asked the president. Mrs. Shilpi Soi was the vice-president and wife of the previous president of the association. She was a short, rotund woman who walked with fitful steps. She couldn't be "switched-off" once she had started talking on a subject. She was supposed to work in close coordination with the president but was mostly found shirking her responsibilities. She had a vile temper, and liked playing dirty politics. "I don't know," said Perzan. "But when I met her last evening, she did say that she would make it," he added.

Dr Shalya presumed that this meant that his V-P was not coming, again. He knew her too well. "If everyone's here, I'd like to call this meeting to order," he announced. It was 11.35 am. "But Atul is not here yet," protested Govind Tulli, the former secretary. Atul Bhandari was 'the' man whose fate had to be decided on that day, and therefore, this high-profile meeting of the 'cabinet'.

"D'Souza, call Atul Bhandari and ask him whether he'll attend," ordered Dr Shalya. He then asked for the minutes of the last meeting to be read out. The senior ladies continued to chirp. Vipasha looked at her watch. They were behind schedule. She was going to have to leave soon. Aparajita had already decided that she would leave around noon whether or not a decision had been taken. She wanted to go shopping.

Tulli began reading, "When the committee last met on October 10, it was decided that a decision ought to be taken on whether to remove Mr Bhandari by collective vote or wait for him to respond to a show-cause notice. To that, the president had said this (the details were mentioned briefly) and Mrs Gorain had said that. Wg Cdr Khanna and Col Aggarwal had raised two separate issues and Mrs Shah had made X suggestion."

A register was now being sent across from one member to another. Each one was required to sign it. "Bhandari Sahib is not responding, Sir," said D' Souza.

"Go to his house then," ordered the president. " The second item on the agenda is the safety and the security of the colony," said Tulli.

"That can be taken up later. I think we ought to resolve Bhandari's case, first and foremost," intervened Col Aggarwal. "Tulli, what does the constitution say?" he asked.

Aparajita and Vipasha looked at each other. The Constitution? Tulli looked at his files. The Constitution was missing! "Ravi, go to House No. 1124, and get the constitution from Mr Khosla," ordered the Wg Cdr "We must co-opt Khosla into the committee. He is very thorough on constitutional matters and can help with legal inputs too," he told the gathering.

"I, too, want to bring in someone into the committee," said Mrs Changkija. "Mrs Kher, who has come into the colony only two years ago, has adopted some of the parks and beautified them. Have you seen the park outside her house? It has become ornamental," she added.

"But didn't she get into a fight with Mr Sabharwal over the pruning of that eucalyptus tree? The police had to intervene. She's an extremist. I oppose her entry," said Vipasha.

"I still believe that she should be co-opted. She's a little high strung but her intentions are okay," insisted Mrs Changkija. "Mrs Gorain, Mrs Shah… what do you say?" she asked, seeking support.

"Well! The last time we had a hot-headed member in this committee, the laying of the sewer pipes got delayed," recalled Mrs Gorain. "I wouldn't want to take that risk again. Anyway, we can discuss that later. At this point, the issue is about Bhandari," she emphasized.

Ravi, D' Souza, Jagdish, Bhurey and the other guards, who had been sent to Bhandari's house, were all missing in action. Meanwhile, Mr Khosla of 1124 walked in. Smiling at everyone, he sat down. He had a paltry crop of silver grey on his head; some hair sprouted from his ears. "Welcome Khosla Sahib! Now that you are here, perhaps you could throw some light on this matter," said Wg Cdr Khanna.

"What matter?" asked Khosla. He had forgotten the document at home. "Didn't Ravi tell you?" asked Vipasha.

Khosla picked up the phone and called home. "Mannu, go to my room, and you will see a file marked JERWA. Bring it to the association office quickly. So, finish what you are doing and then find it. Just come quickly," he commanded gently. "My grandson," he said, by way of explanation. "He is preparing for his upcoming board exams. Bright child but not very hard-working I must say," he added. No one cared. Where was the Constitution and what did it say about such matters?

"From what I remember, we have never before had the occasion to evict someone from the committee. People were decent and diligent and took up responsibility only if they could fulfill it," began Khosla. All eyes were set upon him. "But the right thing to do would be to send him a show-cause notice signed by all committee members and give him one week to respond. Meanwhile, we must issue a circular for a new secretary," he opined.

"There is no one at Bhandari Sahib's house," said D' Souza. He had finally returned.

"So, what took you so long?" asked Dr Shalya.

"Mr Gupte and Group Captain Joshi got into a fight over car parking," offered D' Souza.

"We must do something about this," said Mrs Shah. "People must not be allowed to park anywhere and everywhere. Where are the stickers which were meant to be put up in front of each house?" she asked.

Vipasha looked at Tulli. They were supposed to do this together but had not found time. The telephone by the desk rang. Dr Shalya ignored it. So, the guard from the gate beeped him and said that his wife wanted to talk to him. The president picked up the receiver and said, "Yes. No. Okay. Sure. I don't care. Of course, bitter gourd will do. Yes, I'll be there on time. I don't know," He then smiled weakly. His predicament was self-explanatory.

"About Bhandari, is it okay to draft a letter, Khosla Saab?" asked the president. "Tulli, will you please write it," he requested. The man nodded. He switched on the obsolete computer in the corner and began looking for A4 size paper. There was none. "Ravi, get me some paper," he said.

"I'll have to go to the market. We don't have any left," replied the guard.

"Perzan, could we have some funds please?" asked Tulli. "We also need a stapler, some pens, some glue, some envelopes and a pair of scissors," he noted.

"If Ravi is going, let him also buy some samosas," suggested the Wg Cdr "Dr Sahib, aren't we having some tea?" he asked.

The president called up his disgruntled wife and requested her to organize 15 cups of tea. "Get some biscuits, too," he told Ravi. It was 12.35 pm.

"Ravi, why don't you swing by my house and get me my medicines? I forgot to bring them. I presumed I'd be back sooner," said Mrs Gorain. "Dr Shalya, what about that medical camp we were supposed to have? What happened to that proposal?" she asked. The president looked at Tulli. He had all the answers.

"Oh! That had happened before my time. I think it was handled by Mr Khandelwal of 1050. Then, it moved to Mishraji in 1909. I believe Mrs Mago was also involved in that—Mrs Mago of 258. That file may be here somewhere. Let me check," he said, getting up and unlocking the cupboard. Mannu had, meanwhile, located the file and brought it down to his grandpa.

"Ah, the constitution is here," said Mr Khosla, visibly relieved. But when he opened the file, he discovered that it was the wrong one. Mannu had left by then. He picked up the phone and howled at someone at the other end. "Send the blue file on my table with JERWA clearly written on it. This one says MENWA. Don't these youngsters listen?" he huffed.

"No problem, Khosla Sahib. The tea is here. Have a cup! You'll feel better," said the Col. "But I'll have to take leave now. My son is taking us out to lunch," he explained. Aparajita took the cue and said, "I have an appointment with my dentist. I'd like to excuse myself too." And then Vipasha got up. But Mrs Changkija stopped her. "Stay for a while. The samosas are on their way," she said.

When Ravi returned, he had brought the goodies. It was past 1 pm. Ravenous committee members consumed the hot samosas and gulped down the tea. "That was lunch," said Mrs Shah. "Let me propose something Govind. Why don't you write that letter and have it signed by the president, and send it to Atul's house? If he responds in a week, fine. Otherwise, he shall be booted off this committee," she suggested.

"But the letter has to be signed by everyone on the committee," protested Dr Shalya. He was not going to take the fall for this one. People had already called him an autocrat in the past for some of the decisions that had been taken. His wife called again with an ultimatum. Her parents were waiting for lunch to be served and wanted the Doctor to give them company. "Perhaps we must do this next time. We'll have the letter drafted and meet again next weekend. By then, Khosla Sahib could also tell us about the constitution," he pleaded.

He motioned to get up from his chair when Shilpi Soi breezed into the committee room with a grin and sat herself down. "Sorry I'm late. Just could not get out. Have I missed much?" she asked. Mrs Gorain and Mrs Shah looked at one another. "No. You are just in time. The meeting was scheduled for 11 am. It is only past 1 now," said Mrs Shah sarcastically. The vice-president ignored that and started making enquiries.

"That is impossible. I will not allow this. Atul is a good man and he must be given a chance to explain his situation in person at a meeting. He was really ill, and he needs to be home with his wife, too. I will not sign any show-cause notice, and I don't think anyone here should do so either," she thundered. It was on her suggestion that Atul Bhandari's name had been proposed for the post of the secretary. "Wait. Let me call him," she added.

"Yes Atul, Mrs Soi here. I'm fine. Oh! are you? That's too bad. Okay. Maybe next week. Sure. Come over some time. Bye," she said. People looked at her curiously. "He is home but he's about to leave. His wife has a medical appointment. He'd like to know why he's being harassed. I think we must give him a chance," she insisted.

"He's been absent for nearly six months. I don't think he deserves a chance," retorted Mrs Shah. "And given your record, I don't know if you can bring him around either," she added.

"How dare you talk to me like that?" went Shilpi Soi, training her guns at Mrs Shah.

"Here is the letter. Kindly have a look and advise," intervened Perzan, calmly. In the middle of all that drama, he had discussed the matter with Tulli, and he had typed it out. Then, he quietly locked the safe, and slipped out of the room.

"I put my foot down. This sort of dictatorship will not do," screamed Shilpi Soi. "Ravi, go and get Soi Sahib," she ordered. "No one will move from this place until a decision has been taken," she declared. Ravi did not budge.

Wg Cdr Khanna stirred. "Calm down, Mrs Soi. No one is out to get Bhandari for his lapses. All we wanted was a simple explanation and his response about whether he can perform his duties properly in the future. A large colony such as ours needs a full-time secretary and vice-president. There are many matters to be taken up. Besides, the constitution says that a majority of the committee does have over-ruling authority. I say we issue him a show-cause notice," he offered.

Khosla Sahib got up. "I'm not a member and I must be on my way. I will send across the constitution, though," he said, and left. The senior ladies also pushed their chairs away and got up to make an exit. Wg Cdr Khanna was already on his feet. Vipasha made use of the opportunity and scooted. "I really have to go. I'll support any decision the committee takes," she said. The president was on the phone, telling his wife that he was on his way, and Mrs Soi had found a prey in Govind Tulli. He was patiently putting up with her nonsense.

At 1.40 pm, however, he wrenched himself out of the situation, locked the cupboards, and handed over the keys to D' Souza. "I don't think I'll be participating in future meetings. I'm travelling. And do sort out the issue of the secretary yourself," he told the president. He then walked away, with his mobile phone glued to his ear. The president got up to leave. "Get the constitution from Khosla Sahib's house and bring it to me," he told D'Souza. "And please ensure that we have enough stationery here," he stressed.

D'Souza looked apologetic. "Yes Sir. Of course, Sir," he nodded. The crucial meeting had come to an end. Everything had gone off well. Tea had been served, and biscuits and samosas too. The heater in the room had worked; the computer too. "Barring that incident about the A4 size paper, everything else was okay, don't you think?" he asked Ravi. The guard put away the remaining files into a drawer. "Absolutely, Supervisor Sahib, absolutely. Everything went off well," he said.

****

The Power Trip

His car crawled per force because a vehicle way ahead of him was dragging its wheels, and that had had a cumulative effect. A part of the road on his route was being re-laid, and there was very little scope for overtaking. It was 8 am, and the city had come alive with a vengeance. He honked once or twice and then gave up. It was hot. The air-conditioning had broken down.

The company he worked for belonged to his in-laws. It was a delicate situation. He did not have the fear of a pink slip but there was some pressure to prove his worth. He had recently given up a job with an image consultancy, and had branched out. He had a project in the pipeline, and hoped that the venture would be successful. He had struggled for long enough in his previous grind, and was confident of making a place for himself in an insensate, competitive world.

As he drove, dissembling his contempt for the traffic situation in his city, he thought he saw in a distance, the word 'Accident', as it flashed past him. The trance of the helpless commuter was broken. Malik tried to gather his wits about him. A word had become visible to him for a split second. And then, it was gone. He tried to hunt for it again through the web of people and concrete and the flux but he could not see it.

There was such a flood of information out there. Ideas, concepts, pleas and promos. Bombarding, attacking; rowding the mind. The clutter, the din, the overflow. Was Malik mistaken? 'It must've been an optical illusion. In any case, it's just a word. Let me focus on the road,' he counseled himself.

Then, it came at him yet again, in a whiff. Perhaps he was hallucinating. And just as he recovered, the word reappeared, this time, in sunny yellow. Was it a premonition of a catastrophe? Was someone in the family in danger? Must he call home to check? Or, was he overreacting? He began fidgeting in his seat.

For the most part of the 30 km ride from his home to his workplace, Malik kept seeing the word. There it was… and there it wasn't. Was he disoriented? Was he going to have an accident? Why was the word pounding at him with so much intent? There was no banner or signboard with the word etched on it. Yet, he kept seeing it. Was Malik being forewarned?

Like any prudent driver, Malik became cautious and decided to watch out for the traffic. He didn't want to be caught up in this. He began repeatedly telling himself, 'Let it not be me. Oh please, let it not be me.' He wasn't driving too fast. Just then, the car ahead of him ran into a ghost pedestrian who suddenly came into the picture through a ledge on the divider, and hit him, full on.

Malik put his foot on the brake. He had almost nicked the car ahead, and a truck had nearly rammed into his car. His tail light broke. A crowd gathered. There was a deadlock. Traffic came to a halt and several people got out of their vehicles to have a look. An old man had been hit; he was bleeding severely but was conscious. The driver of the erring car looked aghast. A kind Samaritan helped the injured into his vehicle and they rushed him to a hospital.

There had been an accident and Malik had managed to avoid it by the skin of his teeth. Had the hunch saved him? Had he used the power of his mind to avoid this? A bit shaken and quite preoccupied, he entered a tall, recently-renovated building to go up to his office on the 14th floor. Malikarjun Mitra ran a Public Relations concern along with his sly, duplicitous brother-in-law, Karan. The money for setting this up had come from his father-in-law. It was not the best of situations for Malik, who had put his ambitions before his scruples and agreed to bring Karan on board, among other things.

As he settled down in his cabin and ordered a cup of coffee, he could see a blue file on the table. It was marked 'Top Priority'. This was an account he had been trying very hard to clinch these past few weeks. It was huge. It concerned a prominent European wellness and lifestyle brand that was planning to set up its distribution network in India. It was looking for the perfect PR fit. But this week, too, he had had no success. 'I do wish we can close this today,' he thought. The company where he had previously worked was also angling for this deal. It was a well-known enterprise.

'It would be exhilarating to beat the leaders at their game,' thought Malik. The account was important because of what it stood for. Besides, the funds that would come in would be significant. His partner had already questioned his profit-making abilities and wondered whether now, in the second year of its functioning, the company could show some lucre. 'The client will call me himself today. I just have to be patient. The client will make a move. He will call. I will be chosen over the others,' he began thinking, and throughout the morning, he thought only of this, almost as if he were possessed.

Just after lunch, there was a call on behalf of the clients. "I think they'll go with you," indicated the via-media. Malik had lost some accounts in the past to others with more teeth and more influence. But this positive turn of events was inexplicable. He rushed into a meeting and spoke more than was necessary and promised much more than was possible. Having pocketed a near approval, however, he laid his worries to rest and decided to play his hand. His clients were in the Indian market for good and any publicity would be more than welcome, he concluded. Besides, here was a cash cow that he was going to milk.

He put his best men on the job and ordered them to get cracking. "We must show results," he told them. There was so much to be done; mindsets to be cracked and avenues to be pushed open. He was still grappling with the strategy when a nasty thought pervaded him. 'What if his competitors were to get sucked up in a controversy right now?' That would spoil their chances. 'A scandal for the competition,' thought Malik. 'Give me a scandal,' he pleaded.

Throughout the entire week, the man focused his energies on this one perverse thought. And if I hadn't been privy to this information, I wouldn't have believed it either.

I worked with him during those years. I was one of his many staffers but he was close to me. I knew all his secrets and was even aware of his worst fears and deep insecurities. Malik had roped me in to keep an eye on Karan, and to be an informant. The money was good. I agreed.

Even I could not believe my eyes when one day, the newspapers were awash with an unbelievable scoop. Conversations from tapes seized by one of the law enforcement agencies revealed that the head of the competing Public Relations firm had been lobbying for more than just his fair share of the market. As far as the European clients were concerned, this agency was to be blacklisted. Malik was incredulous with disbelief.

Something abnormal was happening to him. He was ecstatic. "How about getting some of the competitor's major clients to shift over to our agency, eh?" he asked me that morning. How about that? Could this happen just because he wanted it so badly? Was the devil on his side? Malik was on a roll. 'Let me bask in the other's misfortune,' he thought. 'Let me,' he told himself. Malik went about work with the usual pace but his mind was set on seeing his competitor completely deracinated.

I could have tried to reason with him but I did not. Malik's madness paid off. Accounts began coming to us. What was this power that he had acquired? Was he a shaman communicating with something nefarious in the nether world? Were satanic forces at work, for him, with him? He didn't care. Success mattered more than anything else and ethics could be damned! Work began flooding the agency. There was more than what could be managed. Of the many firms in the marketplace, his was the one rising like a phoenix. And he was being watched carefully.

Malik brought more people on board and goaded them to deliver. He also brought in some global experts. This was his big chance and he was determined to break every barrier. He even began wondering if he could buy out his competition. That would be his final victory. He had not told many people that he had been dishonorably discharged from that outfit. They had created the perfect conditions to force him to leave. It hadn't been a part of his plan. There was also the ignominy of having to seek his father-in-law's support and financial help. He had compromised himself. His wife alluded to that every now and then. Karan rubbed his nose in it, too, regularly.

With a tight-fisted father-in-law as chairman, and an incompetent partner as managing director, Malik didn't have real freedom to do what he wished. "What if these two men were to die and leave the company entirely up to me," he asked me one day. I was taken aback. Being greedy about success is not unnatural but wishing for someone to die…wasn't yet my thing.

"Do you know what that would make me?" he asked. I nodded. "Chairman and Managing Director of a reasonably significant market player," he whispered, responding to his own question.

"I don't know… you just seem so overwhelmed by all this that it's beginning to get a little scary now," I confessed.

"Don't you worry! Just follow my cue and we'll crack this one. Are you with me?" he asked. I didn't have a choice. So, I did his bidding and kept his negativity company.

I was scouring for information on the competitor's exact financial status and culling out other useful details and passing it on to the man. Besides that, there was the routine task of executing plans for existing clients. But Malik began using his days to plan something diabolical. He was going to usurp power, and he was willing to pay a price…any price.

Continuing on his lunatic streak, Malik began focusing his energies on his thoughts, somehow believing that he could get this done. "There will be death in the family. These men will die," he told me. He rolled that thought over and over in his mind until he feared he might end up blurting it out loud. Then, one day, the old man fell ill. Doctors said they couldn't make out what was wrong with him. There were no physical indicators and the test results revealed nothing serious. Perhaps, a change of environment would help. Perhaps, a holiday.

Malik felt a wicked smile creep up around the corners of his mouth. Was he really able to send out such powerful thoughts into space? Soon after that, Karan was seriously injured in a freak motor-cycle crash. Both obstacles were down. Malik felt a volcanic surge of energy within him; the lava would consume everyone in its path. He could feel it move through his veins and pervade every little molecule in his body. He was alive, alert and powerful. His mind was agile, and his system, in top gear. He had played a conscious role in all this. It had not been an involuntary process.

There was just one thing on his agenda now—ensuring that these men were dead. The stentorian voice in his head grew louder and louder with every passing day and he could think of nothing else. The ugly head of everything that was brutal and merciless and cold-blooded, dominated him. He decided that the time to launch Plan A had come. He was going to suggest taking the chairman and his partner to their home in the hills for total recovery and rest. He would arrange for an in-house doctor and a nurse. I was to tag along.

His wife protested but he had his way. "We also have some important decisions to take about the company's expansion. Spending time together will resolve everything. You don't understand," he chided her. The woman gave him a dyspeptic smile. He had seemed a little strange of late; somehow more assertive, more aggressive and definitely more diplomatic with her. She insisted on coming along. "While you discuss plans, I'll take care of the house for you," she offered. He denied her request.

On D Day, he took great care packing. The car had been serviced. We began driving up to the chairman's summer home. Malik was hopeful about his agenda. He wasn't sure how well his plan would work out but the word 'Murder' kept haunting him. Did he really intend to carry out his task? Did he have no qualms? Was there no way out? It did seem like an awful risk to take. In a span of just a few months, he had gone from being an ordinary man to one who was irrevocably obsessed.

"So, why do you think we must expand at this juncture?" his father-in-law had asked throughout the journey. "Isn't it too early? Besides, how do we know that Xim Communications is up for grabs?" he had probed. Malik had tried every sort of response although the answer was really simple. He wanted to grow big, really big, and he wanted some more funds. He had argued fiercely but there had been no headway. The old man was shrewd.

Malik decided to put off his plans until later. The word

flashed by him, again. That familiar word! We had been climbing uphill for the last hour or so, and were about 46 kms from our destination. The driver parked by the side and got out of the vehicle to stretch his legs. Malik and I, we both stepped out, too. We took in the fresh air and looked at the scenery in front of us. Malik then walked away from the vehicle for a bit. A nurse was checking the chairman's pulse. The old man was on the phone. Karan had dozed off.

There was a slight cloud cover over the mountain and it seemed like it could rain. At a decisive moment, as per his plan, he would, thought Malik ... But just as he was about to turn around to return to the car, a herd of bulls came rushing out at him from the curve below on the narrow road. There might have been about 35 or 40 of them; running at top speed, as if they were frightened of something. One of them rammed right into him. Their nervous herder was tearing after them with a stick, shouting and screaming. Malik plunged into the abyss below; his eyes wide open in shock; his mind, numb... completely numb.

****

Qaidi No 48

She was a tall, light-skinned, well-built woman with rippling biceps and well-toned muscles, like those of a wrestler. The left side of her face bore burn marks and she had a scar that ran down the middle of her left cheek all the way into her neck and shoulder blade. She was completely bald. Yet, she did not look hideous. She was prisoner No. 48. She was called Bai Sa, out of respect, perhaps.

As I was pushed into the cell, crammed with a hundred or more women in it, it was her that I first noticed. She seemed regal, with the many beads around her neck, biceps and wrist, and her cold, steely gaze. Some women prisoners sat by her feet, and others stood in attendance. She did not speak, and it was mostly through finger movements and a twitch of her eyebrows that she got work done. Even the jail staff was deferential to her. No one seemed to question her authority.

Bai Sa must have been fifty-five. They said she had been at the prison since the very beginning. Her legend was such that there were several stories on when and how she had been brought and incarcerated there. One of these indicated that she had come in as a twenty-something into this prison for having committed hara-kiri in her region. They drew dreadful tales of the number of men she had slain. They also believed that she would die here. They said she was from the Bhil community, a tribe from the forests of Gir in Gujarat. Another said she had come in during her early thirties, and that she was a celebrated contract killer from Dhoomanganj in Allahabad. Here again, there were colourful stories of her exploits and deeds.

I gathered all this, by and by, but for the moment…Bai Sa looked at me. One of the women egged me on, saying, "Go on. Pay your obeisance, and introduce yourself." I shuffled a bit, before moving forward to touch her feet. She made no move. I was expected to start talking now. I felt the presence of several pairs of eyes on me, watching me intently, and waiting for me to say something. After all, I was the new entrant, and a young one, at that.

"My name is Baruni. I am 21," I said. Bai Sa pulled at her hookah pipe and let out some smoke, waiting for me to go on. "I hail from village Duko in Ghaghra from the Gumla district in Jharkhand," I continued. There was a murmur. Someone else in that cell must have been from my state, too.

"So, why are you here?" asked an aide. I kept quiet. "Tell us why you are here," she repeated. Their leader waited patiently. She was wearing a white saree with a blue border. Her shoulders were bare. She wasn't wearing a blouse.

"I was caught by the Ranchi police after I killed someone," I said. It was a cold, premeditated murder. I was still at home after I had committed it, and gave myself up when the police came in. In a small village, word spreads fast.

"So, whom did you knock off? Such a young girl…I wouldn't have imagined. The lass has guts," said one of Bai Sa's close aides. I later found out that her name was Purna.

"I poured petrol over my brother-in-law while he was asleep and burnt him alive," I said. There was more murmuring in the cell. I had their complete attention now. They inched closer to where I was standing. Some of the prisoners had even brought their hands up to their mouth and covered it, aghast. Others looked on, surprised. Purna spoke up. "Tell us more. Why did you do that?" she asked.

I took a deep breath. Unfortunately, I would have to relive the entire episode. "He was a horrible man. He had made my sister miserable. He repeatedly stole the money she earned. He did not care about their three children. He was an alcoholic. Of late, he had started beating her recklessly. But when he attacked her for the nth time, and branded her with a hot rod for protesting, I had had enough," I said. A cell mate put her hand on my shoulder, to convey empathy.

"Your poor sister," she whispered. "This is the fate of us uneducated women. We have no one to go to. We have no money. And, if the husband turns out to be a useless lout, this is what we have to suffer," she added.

I thought of my sister, Lakhi. She did not have the courage to retaliate or fight that monster but I wasn't like that. "I did what I had to do, fully aware of the consequence. Given the opportunity, I would kill him again. There is absolutely no remorse," I concluded.

Bai Sa said nothing. Instead, she spat something she had been chewing, and looked away. The durbar was to be disbanded. She was going to rest. The women ushered me from her. Purna held me by my elbow, and herded me to another spot. "So, you just killed him?" she asked again. I nodded. "And, what did your sister feel about it?" she prodded. I don't know whether Lakhi would thank me for what I had done or hate me for the rest of our life. She was one of those pathetic women who were content that they had a husband, even if he turned out to be a blood-sucking leech; completely irresponsible, unstable and unemployable.

"You know, I'm curious about that woman. Tell me more about her," I asked of Purna.

"You mean Bai Sa? Don't let anyone catch you calling her "that woman" or you'll have hell to pay. She doesn't like being spoken about. But I can tell you this—try not to annoy her," Purna responded, before lying down and shutting her eyelids. I sat by her, my back to the gruff wall, thinking of my sister and of the plight of her children. What would they do now? Where would they go? Later that day, there was word that Bai Sa had summoned me.

"She already likes you. Lucky girl! Don't contradict her and don't talk unless you are spoken to," advised Purna as I was guided to Bai Sa's cell. It was at the other end of the zenana (women's) wing and it was massive. It had a large wooden bed with a thick mattress and a clean blue batik print bedsheet and several bolsters and cushions. There was a tall pedestal fan at the head of the bed; a small refrigerator on the other side, and several boxes with betel nut and tobacco strewn carelessly on a table by the bed, and a nut cracker.

She motioned me to sit down. I squatted on the floor. She then asked her hangers-on to leave. "Come closer!" she said. I stood up gawkily. What was she going to do to me?

I went up to her rather slowly and kept standing. She asked me to come up and sit on the bed. I was beginning to get nervous. "Tell me more about yourself," she said. I looked at my feet, awkwardly. It was almost like being scrutinized by someone of the opposite sex. "There is nothing much to say," I responded.

"You have a sweet voice. Do you sing?" she asked. I nodded.

"I used to hum as a teenager but…" I managed to say.

"Come now! Sing for me," she ordered. I hesitated. "Sing for me now," she hissed. I knew that there was no other way out. I began singing for her. She stroked my arm for a while, and just as I was beginning to get all worked up, she lay back, and shut her eyes. Within no time, she had fallen asleep. That is how I ended up becoming her personal assistant and favourite aide.

I now had clout with the jail authorities, and could get away with a lot. We had an endless supply of booze (I took up drinking like a pro) and tobacco, and of films (porn, of course) and music CDs (with the trippy sort of stuff; very marijuana... Hmm Mmm.) One day, a GLOCK 17 9mm Safe-Action Pistol made its way into the cell. Bai Sa summoned me and asked me to start practicing. "Someone will show you where to practice. I want you to be ready in six months," she commanded.

Things had moved with lightning speed for me. From being miserable to being imprisoned to being "upgraded' and now being pampered. I was personally trained to shoot by some of the staff. I practiced for over four hours, five days a week at an empty warehouse about ten kilometres from the prison. The ammunition was provided for. Someone took me there every morning. I even got extra meat, bananas and biscuits to eat. Rum was de rigueur.

With time, I got better at shooting. I had even begun to enjoy it. I had no idea about the why, where and when of the future of the firearm. But for the moment, this was it! I waited impatiently for the day when she'd send me word that I was to assassinate someone, somewhere. I did not even need a reason for wanting to kill someone. It was exciting to be given that kind of power and immunity. My training continued. I wasn't sure of whether the higher ups were aware of what was happening in their prison.

In the months that followed, as I waited for something eventful to happen to me, I was sent for riding lessons, as well. Every Sunday, one of the wardens would come very faithfully to my cell at 4 am, and escort me to a jeep waiting outside the premises. We'd then be on the road for about an hour before hitting a ranch, where, much to my discomfort, I was made to ride. I despised it. But no amount of clamouring worked with Bai Sa. She just flicked off my complaints like she did the flies that sat on her arm.

A year passed by, and I was still toiling, purposelessly. There was no grand objective to the hard work and no results to show, either. I was getting frustrated. I had been primed up so well that I needed some sort of outlet. My cell mates and "friends" had begun asking me if my "mission" was over. Having to look away from them without a response was agonizing for a fully "charged" young "assassin". Besides, my "baptism" hadn't yet happened. I really couldn't call myself that.

When I had had enough, I decided to confront Bai Sa about it. I wasn't as afraid of her as all the others, and that made the task less fearsome. One night, I sought her audience, and waited my turn. We normally stayed in the vicinity of her quarters and someone would beckon us in. I had smoked a series of *beedis* as I hung about near her cell, awaiting that call. It did not come. I was told that she was far too tired and had retired for the night. This continued for a fortnight. I got agitated. Besides, I heard from others who were close to her that she wasn't planning to see me for quite some time that month.

That was it! I lost my patience, picked up my pistol and stormed into her cell. It was already 9 pm and things were winding down for the night. Two of her aides were by her side. One was at her feet, pressing them. The other was mixing something in a bowl. Wait! Was that a medicine? Was Bai Sa ill? Or, was it a drug? Whatever be the case, I was not going to relent.

I motioned for both the aides to leave the area. They had seen the pistol. They left without a word. I sat myself down on a stool by her head, and waited for her to wake up. She did not stir much through the night. I kept dozing, as well. But at about 2 am, she turned sides and asked for some water. Her eyes widened with genuine surprise when she saw me put a glass to her lips.

"How is my favourite girl?" she asked in a voice that was so frail that it seemed to belong to a child. She had lost a lot of weight and the veins in her neck stood out. Her scar had become prominent and her eyebrows had become faint. "And why is she carrying her weapon around with her?" she added. I turned my head away, slightly ashamed. I had intended to bully her into telling me what she was preparing me for, and why I was being trained so severely. Instead, I found myself looking at her with genuine affection and regard.

"How's the training?" she asked, as if she did not know. I nodded mildly, saying nothing. I was sulking. She had obviously been well informed about the training because she had never called me before to check on it. She would have been given a day by day account of what I was doing and how I had fared. Her well-wishers in jail would've have been more than happy to have done that for her. She was only trying to amuse me. I knew that. And, I was torn between letting it all out and keeping my calm. But for her, I'd have been languishing in some corner of that jail, going through a drab routine, and wishing I were dead, perhaps.

I did realize that she had, in that sense, given me a new lease of life. She had made it interesting and exciting and adventerous, and given me something edgy to look forward to. I couldn't get myself to let off steam. I opened my mouth and thought of saying something a little sensible and mature but nothing came out. I fiddled with the bedcover, digging my nails deep into the cloth, and looking helter-skelter. I thought I'd just better go. I didn't have it in me yet to take her on. I'd have to come back another night, more prepared.

Seeing me fidget, she somehow understood my state of mind. She held my hands in hers, and said, "I'm not going to be around for much longer. I'm unwell." My eyes must have conveyed my complete surprise at that revelation. I nearly jumped. "Oh! But that can't be so, Bai Sa. What do you mean?" I asked, utterly shocked. My eyebrows had furrowed in, and I looked at her for an explanation.

She strengthened her grip on my hand, pulling me back. "Sit down! Sit down! I should have told you this earlier. I have been unwell for a while now," she confessed. I remained surprised. She continued. "I wanted to look after you. I also wanted you to be empowered enough to look after yourself after I'm gone," she said faintly. I couldn't believe what I was hearing. She knew that she was going to die, and had taken it upon herself to look after me. There was really no familial bond between us. And...yet!

I found myself taking deep breaths. "Use the skill well when they release you," she said, patting me on my cheek. I found myself smiling lightly. "You never know, you could even teach other people something if you learn it well yourself. So, don't be slack about it!" she cautioned me. Did she mean that? Was she actually suggesting that I stay on the right side of the law? Why would she have put a gun in my hand? Was she really going to abandon me? I looked at her for answers. The softness of her gaze astounded me. It was clean and pure, almost motherly. I kissed her goodnight, and staggered back to my quarters.

I was overcome by an unknown feeling. She was going to perish, and that was breaking my heart. On the other hand, it was also as if a huge weight had been lifted off of my shoulders. Did I still want to be an assassin? Was I drunk on that possibility? Or, was I going to change? Would I try to fit into mainstream society? I had a skill now and that could be put to definite use. Was I going to do that? As I held my arm out, and tried to reach my future, I felt a tingling in my bones. There was something entirely unknown to look forward to…on the horizon… far, far away. And, the choice would be entirely mine!

****

Shocking Pink

The pink of her shocking pink saree was, to say the least, very shocking. Standing right next to her, as we posed for photographs, and being pushed together by the jostling crowd of students surrounding us, I did think that the ghastly colour would rub off on my clean, white dress. My spotless, pristine, untarnished new dress. I don't remember who had bought it for me or why, but I do remember feeling undeniably immaculate in it. Virgin fresh.

I had been invited to a college deep down south and far away from my comfort zone in the north to speak to students there about how to recover from grievous injuries—mentally, emotionally and physically. I had been in a car crash some years ago. I had gone flying through the windscreen, crashed into a newly-tarred road, got hit by a speeding motorbike and was partially crushed by the wheels of a one-ton truck. It had been quite a ride! I had then come back to the mainstream and won a local municipal election.

But when the incident happened, I had had dozens of broken bones, a shattered spine, a dislocated shoulder, an excoriated ankle and a hundred stitches on my face. I was covered with scars and wounds. There had been undeniable trauma in the family. For a week after the crash, I wasn't even aware of what I had gone through. I would come out of a trance, sometimes to see friendly, anxious faces stare at me and at other times to be conscious of men and women in white and blue and green amble around.

I mostly remained unconscious. It was a calm, soothing pit. I was alone, undisturbed and unchallenged. No demands, no expectations, no formalities, no lies. No duties, no responsibilities, no pressures, no ties. Nowhere to get to; nothing to accomplish; no emotional rollercoasters, no reconciliations to handle. Just a recurring pain and then, a blackout. Some normalcy and then, a fade-out. Was I dead or was I alive? Could I feel? Or, was it over? Quite an experience!

Following several months of treatment, I used a pair of crutches. A machine held up my spine. It still does. And, there were scars on my face. They still show. They shock people who are curious. Part entertainment. Part anecdote. There is a long mark that cuts through my bushy eyebrows and goes all the way up to my forehead with a slant towards the left temple. The other scar is over my right ear; the lobe is gone.

My lower lip is cut in two and even though the doctors worked hard on me, there is a gap that shows and makes me look different. My teeth have all but gone; shattered by the impact. But I'm not a joke; not a very cruel one at least. I adjust my dentures and continue to ponder. In this particular moment, however, all I'm concerned about is whether the pink of the woman's saree has rubbed off on me. We're both unbearably hideous in our own ways, I reckon. And, hideously unbearable, too.

But this is information that we share only among ourselves. It is the unspoken dialogue of 'the broken' and 'the repaired'. She knows that I know that she knows what I feel. The slight discomfort with the self in spite of the glory. The need to make minor adjustments just to liberate the mind. The desire for balance, for lucidity and for normality. She has them sporadically just as I have them, too. Or so, I presume.

I know I'm supposed to motivate everyone in front of me by saying that we always recover from accidents. Perhaps we do. Or then, perhaps, we don't. Perhaps, not entirely.

We might be reborn, re-invented and re-done. To recover from an injury to the mind might take Herculean effort. My mind is irresolute. I can see that it likes drawing from the negative as much as it does from the positive. It has now taken the pink from all my raw flesh and has embedded that into my sub-conscious. I can often see blood and bone and torn muscles and shattered ligaments everywhere. I hallucinate. I am spinning yarns. My mind has a mind of its own!

I know that I have to now open my mouth and say something motivating. "Be positive! Failure is a part of life. Get up after a fall! Never give up! When the going gets tough…the tough…" and the rest of it. Everyone's waiting. Hanging by every second. Looking forward to these "words of wisdom". Eager pairs of eyes are looking up at the podium. They want me to talk.

But I can't. Not just yet. I look at the eucalyptus trees around me in the huge campus. Some have been planted right in the middle of the pavement. Or, vice versa. They've had cement poured on them; around their roots, and all over their base. Some may have been uprooted from one spot and re-planted elsewhere. I hear them sigh. They seem to be gauging me, too. At some distance, I can see clutches of bamboo that have crowded out the other plants and seem to be spreading arbitrarily.

I look at the walls at the far end of the compound towards the main road. Some Gods have descended upon the area to save the walls from being treated as urinals. I can feel abject disgust. I look at the alleyways behind the campus. I think of dark nights, of psychedelic drugs, of cat and mouse games, of night watchmen and of beggars, of roads that must be eerie at that hour; of prostitutes doing their business there and of the police, doing their work, of course.

The woman in the pink saree is looking at me too. I wonder what she's thinking. Where could she be from? What might her story be? Could it be far more inspiring than mine? Perhaps she has combatted genuine repression and come out victorious. Perhaps she's had her freedom snatched away by merciless traffickers. Perhaps she escaped from terrorists and arsonists from a land quite far away. Perhaps she deserves every accolade that she is about to receive. Perhaps I must not push her off the dais. Perhaps I must not even think about it.

But…what if I were to push her off the dais! Would that be so wrong, so unpardonable? Would that get me into trouble, serious trouble? I could simply hobble up to her, congratulate her, shake her hand and then, give her a shove? I would, not to mention, have to be careful about maintaining my own balance. After all, I wouldn't want to tumble over with her. That isn't the idea as you now know.

'What leads you to come up with these thoughts,' you ask. I have already softly told you that it is the mind. Mine has a plan of its own. Even I cannot control the machinations of my own mind. Can you control yours? In any case, all my focus is now on the woman present on the dais with me. She must have done something truly remarkable to be sitting there.

What if she has saved the lives of a hundred people, maybe more? What if there had been an explosion in a ravine? Or, in a mine? What if she had lost those limbs pulling out survivors? What if she was attacked by a wild animal in the forest? And what of her children? Did she get that trying to save them? Or, could she have tried fending off child molesters? That would get my vote, too. Women and children! Depraved men will do just about anything to them.

Should I instead look for a man to send flying off the dais? There was that one man who had helped me on to the dais. How about him? He looked simple, even ordinary. What about his touch, though? Was that simple, even ordinary? Did he hold my forearm just a tad more intimately than was desired? Did his fingers brush past my side just where my breasts curved?

Could he become the representative of all the men who

have rubbed me (pun intended) the wrong way all my life? Could he be punished for everyone else? Could he take the brunt for the man who crashed into my car those many years ago? Could he quell my rage? Would it be enough to push him off the dais? Would it be alright to do so? Why couldn't I let it go? Why wouldn't I let it go? I had survived. Some would say I had even flourished.

But the pink is just too much for me to handle. Those memories of torn open skin and cut up flesh. All that blood. So much blood. Enough to drown out this campus. Enough to drive me crazy. Pushing me to the brink of insanity. Goading me to go on. Provoking me to give in. Spurring me on. Inviting me. Asking me not to stop. Not now. Coaxing me to try it out. Wanting me to flip. I am wide-eyed. I'm listening to the voices in my head. I'm shouting back at them. I want to be calm. I want to be calm.

There's a question. What if he is one of the nice guys? Would I still want to push him off the dais? What if he doesn't deserve this? What if he is a single father to four children? Or, if he has an invalid wife at home? Waiting for him. What if he's working two jobs to make enough money for the house? What if he was like the man who called for help while I lay on the road, disintegrated, that fateful night?

What if?

So, I lose my footing a bit. People rush to help. I feel bony fingers holding me; taking my weight, at the back. I turn around. Very slowly. It's a young girl. Comely. A student. She has been positioned behind me just in case I trip. Or fall. And, she has been alert all along. She steadies me. Gives me a smile. "Are you okay, Ma'am?" she asks. "Yes," I tell her. I am okay now. And then, I deliver my speech.

****

The Heiress

He has been in a coma for nineteen days, and I don't know whether he'll survive.

Harilal Deensukh Nadoda is an obdurate man; an employer intensely despised by his staff. Although his parents had named him Harilal Deensukh or 'Gods child, who would bring happiness', he makes everyone's life miserable, and quite effortlessly too. No one likes him and almost everyone is wary of him. This includes his business partners and acquaintances. The man is temperamental and egotistical.

Harilal was an ambitious block printer when he began his career forty-five years ago. He gradually became the largest wholesale producer and seller of printed bed sheets in west India. He has a booming business, and his shops and factories are spread out in Ahmedabad, Surat and Baroda. For most part of the month, he remains at his headquarters in Ahmedabad where he has a showroom and a godown at Teen Darwaja, and another shop in the Dhal Garwad market. More recently, he bought a shop in the C G market and stocked it with silk Patola sarees.

Harilal sits in his showroom at Dhal Garwad all day from eleven in the morning to eight in the evening, making life hell for all his employees. For someone hitting 80, he is extremely active, though; walking up and down the showroom, spread over 1,500 square feet, and over three floors. He is flat-footed and has a slight problem with his right leg. He hobbles through his fiefdom, nit-picking, criticizing and bullying everyone. Workers who do not pause to acknowledge him when he enters their workshop get ticked off. Those who set work aside to do so are admonished. There is no protocol and no 'correct' reaction.

We normally keep georgette and embroidered sarees on the ground floor and hand block printed cotton sarees on the first floor. But, once in a while, he will shake the place upside down, and reverse that order, without reason. At other times, the basement, which is a large storage space, will be disturbed. The showroom's rear entrance leads to a workshop where wooden blocks are made. Even this space, which should ideally be left untouched, because of the sheer number of equipment there, and the delicate nature of block making and printing, is often disrupted.

If you visit Dhal Garwad, Lalaji will be found standing over a block printer, his back sticking out like that of a rotund duck, shouting at him for not doing it quite right. Just the other day, it was my turn to be in the firing line.

I am originally from Pethapur, close to Gandhinagar. My family has been in the block making business for nearly a century. Both my father and my grandfather have served Lalaji. So, I was sent to work for him, as well. I take a bus from Gandhinagar at 7 am and travel 29 kilometers to Ahmedabad to be able to reach the showroom before nine. If anyone is late by even one minute, he chops off half our pay for the day. Reasoning with him or with his cronies is futile.

In the past, blocks would be made at Pethapur and transported to Ahmedabad, but of late, Lalaji has shifted that to this workplace. We use teak wood, known as Sagwan, which is sourced from Valsad near the Gujarat Maharashtra border. Teak is strong; it is a great base for carving and it does not absorb water or distort in shape and size. We cut pieces of the wood and paint it white and then trace the required design on to it. For that, we use a hand drill involving a bow or Kamthi and a driller called Saarardi, and chisel out the fine shapes.

The work is intricate and painstaking. Sometimes, we carve blocks with lines that are but a millimeter thin. We must also account for the fact that the designs in these blocks must allow for up to four colours to be printed on fabric. Most blocks take two to three days to make and some take up to a week. I am reasonably skilled. So, I find myself working on the toughest and the most challenging blocks, and I'm expected to churn them out like a machine.

On that fateful day, I was working on one of the more intricate blocks, which had both star patterned motifs and abstract floral ones on it. That was tedious, but I was humming to myself when I felt the hair on my back stand, as if some negative energy had pervaded the area. I continued to work but felt some consternation within my fellow workers too. But taking a break or lifting one's eyes off one's work was scoffed at in this factory by Lalaji and his spies.

This discomfort lingered for a while. So, I put down my tools to see that the old man had just walked into the courtyard. Behind him was a young girl, dressed in the most outrageous orange dress that was a cross between a skirt and a pair of harem pants. It ballooned up as she walked by as if it was full of helium. She also wore a hideous black top, with spaghetti straps. I found myself staring at her with contempt and disgust. But my gaze was misconstrued; not by the young lass but by the old geezer himself. The oddly dressed girl was his granddaughter.

"Hey! You! Yes…you…Tamarum nam sum che? (What's your name?)" he demanded angrily.

"Madhukar, Lalaji," I replied, in my best voice. "What do you do here?" he asked.

"I'm a block maker, Lalaji. I'm Kanubhai's son and Navjibhai's grandson," I introduced myself. He showed no signs of recognition. And, this, after my family had served him for so long. In fact, my father was an award winning block maker. "Come to my office at once," he ordered and trotted away. The girl followed. She was mocking me, as if she knew that I was in for a jobation.

When I entered his office, she was there, seated on her grandpa's chair and playing with a paper weight. Grandpa Harilal had put himself down on a sofa on the other side of the small cabin. "How dare you stare at my *pautri*?" he said, coming straight to the point.

"But Lalaji, I wasn't staring," I protested.

"Oh, but you were," intervened the young thing.

I felt humiliated. I was indeed gaping at her but I wished that I could tell both of them that it was shock and disapproval that they saw in my eyes, not appreciation or desire. But I needed that job and I could do nothing else. I wasn't ambitious and I did not want to migrate to a bigger city. Therefore, I was destined to serve my time. No one, not even my own father, had ever hauled me up. And these two were determined to punish me. Vexed and cornered, I surrendered.

"I'm sorry, Lalaji. It won't happen again," I assured them, and left the room, quite indignant. 'I wish they too feel insulted like this, some day,' I cursed (the poor have no other ammunition), and went back to my block. I had been drilling cylindrical holes into it, connecting the upper side to the lower surface, when the unfortunate episode took place. I picked it up again. The holes help free the air bubbles and the excess paste while printing. 'I wish I could run this drill through the head of that haughty girl,' I muttered to myself. Why did I set eyes on her in the first place?

Anyway, after the incident, I decided to be more careful. I also presumed that I had seen the last of her. But the week after, 'the princess' strolled into the work area, again. She looked carefully at the blocks that had been soaked in oil. That is done for about a fortnight as it softens the grains in the timber. Then, she walked past the rectangular printing tables. Sarees had been stretched out on some. She looked at me immodestly, challenging me to ogle her again, but I didn't. This routine was repeated for many days. It was asphyxiating to have her hover around.

Meanwhile, Lalaji made an important announcement. His granddaughter, Vidhi, who had finished her studies, was going to be groomed to take over the business from him. Preparations began for the big event which was to take place on the last day of the Navratri puja. We were all going to be tossed from the frying pan into a raging fire. Vidhi was even more vindictive than her old man; the gene must run in the family. Soon after the announcement, she began sauntering into the premises with great authority, initiating changes and shooting orders like pellets off an air gun. People were beginning to get somewhat annoyed.

Lalaji had guarded his homegrown business steadfastly for at least four decades and had finally decided to entrust it to another person. Even his sons had been kept out of the day-to-day management—playing but a marginal, secondary role—sourcing material and coordinating shipments and orders. They weren't involved in the finances and never participated in crucial meetings. But this young girl had come and usurped power overnight, without even giving us time to get acclimatized to her style of torture. It was nerve-wrecking. She was also speaking of downsizing and of modernizing. But hadn't she tried her hand at modeling and failed? Or, so it was rumoured.

I began dreading her visits. Even when she was not around, her spies were at work. One could not say anything openly. It was as gruelling as a boot camp. Lunch and tea breaks were strictly monitored. Some of my colleagues got 'converted' into stooges. I remember mentioning something about her horrible dress sense during a tea break, and word got around. I had also remarked that she had an awful voice that could cut through the toughest of metals. I was hauled up the next morning for stepping out of line, and cautioned.

"This is your second warning, Madhukar," said Raval, Lalaji's right hand man. Raval had been with this family from the very beginning—he was a Man Friday. He did everything and he knew everyone. In fact, he also had duplicate keys to the safe at the factories and at home. He was that trusted. Raval looked at me with disdain, and grunted, "One more error like this...and you'll be out, Madhukar. Lalaji won't care that your father and your grandfather worked for him. So, beware!" I knew I should have been prudent.

Meanwhile, I heard from friends in Pethapur that renowned Hindi film director Tarang Rindani was to visit Ahmedabad soon. He was scouting for a heroine for his next great project, *Padmini*, based on the story of the beautiful, brave, legendary (perhaps mythical) 14th century Rajput queen from Chittor. Rindani's last biopic, *Swayamvar*, had been a blockbuster, grossing almost Rs 111 crore, if newspaper reports could be believed.

"Rindani will be here throughout the Navratras," I announced at tea break, the following day. My fellow workers began taking interest. "Really? Who told you so?" asked one. "It is in the papers. Haven't you noticed?" I responded. They shook their heads. "He is looking for a beautiful Gujarati girl with charismatic screen presence," I said. "Auditions will be held at the Jai Shankar Sundari Hall on Haveli Road in Raikhad," I added. A cousin of mine was planning to try her luck.

"Vidhi Behn should also try. How marvelous it would be to become a film star! Imagine the kind of money to be made! The fame! The popularity! It is much more than people make walking the ramp," I stressed. I must admit that the heiress was good-looking—about 5'5" tall, slim, olive-skinned, light-eyed and with healthy, long, black, straight hair.

"C'mon! C'mon! You gossip mongers! Time is up. Don't you have work to do?" Raval intervened. "Moreover, we'll be having a ceremony where Lalaji wants to make a huge announcement, and we must prepare for that," he prodded. Seven days went by. Our shop in the Dhal Garwad market was rather large and spacious. It was to be decorated from top to bottom for the very first time in its history.

The old man continued to harass us. We worked from

morning till midnight—running errands, picking up and dropping things, skipping meals and not getting enough sleep. Some of us had to stay back and work into the night. I was one of them. Finally, D-day arrived. The office was wiped spic and span. Lalaji's business associates were to descend upon us. Vidhi was to be appointed the new czarina, or so went the buzz. But with no formal training and no experience? The patriarch was going senile!

We were huddled into the courtyard and Lalaji began his lecture. It was laced with self-aggrandizement and a lot of malarkey. (He was successful because we—the workers—had given the business our blood and sweat.) But he spoke of how he began 60 years ago with nothing to fall back on, which was false. He had wormed out money from his wife's father and bullied his own father into granting him his inheritance.

"I would go from showroom to showroom, looking for work. I walked miles on end, without food or water. I began with small orders, and gradually built these shops, brick by brick. And, look where I have reached today," he boasted. "The honesty and the hard work have paid off," he stressed. Yes… our hard work and …honesty? Bah! Everyone knew how shrewd and manipulative the old tyrant was. "And, today, I hope to bring in someone equally capable to share my burden," he announced, smugly.

His granddaughter hadn't arrived at the venue yet. Her late night dances at the *Raas* had been taking a toll. Besides, she was at the beauty parlour. I was assigned to take her there and then bring her to the shop. It was already 10.30 am. We were running late. When she eventually turned up, with her face heavily painted and looking very much a geisha, in a garish purple skirt and a really tiny backless shocking pink bodice, I had to prevent myself from flinching and telling her the truth.

"So, how do I look?" she asked. "Very nice, Behn," I lied.

"Do you know that I met Rindani at the audition?" she asked. I nodded comprehensively (with the head rolling from top to bottom and from side to side). "He thinks that I could be his next new find. He wants me to go to Mumbai with him," she declared. "Do you think I should take this up?"

I was flummoxed. "Who am I to say anything, Madam? It is your decision," I proffered.

"But of one thing, I am certain," I said. "If you became a star, that would put Gujarati actresses on the national map, and who knows, even on the international platform someday. Everyone would know what we are made of. That thought by itself makes me very, very proud to be a Gujarati," I submitted. Her eyes twinkled. (I had managed to brainwash her.) We reached the venue, and Vidhi walked up very awkwardly in her high heels to the podium.

Lalaji brought her up to the dais and announced, "I had never thought that I would hand over the business to anyone while I was still alive. I couldn't let my sons take over, and my daughters are busy with their own lives." His progeny shifted in their seats, visibly embarrassed. "I am not keen to give it to a professional manager either. This is a family business, and that's how it will stay. But then, Vidhi came home after finishing her studies," he said, softening up, and looking at his granddaughter, who seemed to be looking elsewhere.

"Over the past few months, she has shown that she has what it takes to handle these operations. She has been observing everything, and seems ready to take over. Therefore, it is with great pleasure and much anticipation that I present to you my heir, and your new owner and master. Serve her as you have served me! She will make a great leader, and take our businesses forward," he declared. There was a feeble applause with Raval goading everyone to make some noise. He then invited the new boss to say a few words.

Vidhi took to the mike. Everyone waited for her words of wisdom. "I've had a smashing time here," she began. "I've danced at the *Raas*, and feasted a lot," she noted.

Some of us in the audience smiled. Yes, we were aware of that. But no one anticipated her next words. "And now, I'm going to Mumbai." She wasn't making any sense. The old fox was stunned. Was this an acceptance speech?

Raval quickly slunk up to Vidhi on stage, and whispered something in her ear. She looked at him, completely unperturbed. Allaying his fears and motioning him to go back to his place, she asked, "Oh! about the business?" And then she added, "Sorry, Baapji. But this doesn't excite me at all. I have far better things to do. You should have really just handed it over to my father."

Harilal Deensukh Nadoda collapsed on the ground, clutching his chest. He went pale and began sweating profusely. His pupils dilated and he had the most incredulous look on his face. The humiliation must've been too much for him to handle. He went into a shock, and later, slipped into a coma. And, I seriously do not know whether he'll survive!

****

The Pursuit

Through the haze and through the fog, that night, Sejal heard him sprinting after her, at a safe distance, but nevertheless…there. His feet trampled old, dry branches on their way through the forest just as hers had. Miles and miles of forest; lush green at most places and a little jaded at others but always dense and really cold. The lushness helped her make her escape. Or so she thought at the time.

On a sombre, gloomy night—one that was darker than those that had preceded it, Sejal had decided to abandon her lover, and run away. But he had stirred just as she was about to make an exit. His large, brown eyes stared into hers. That look! How often, in the past, had she given up her heart to that gaze! It was sensual and passionate, yet caring. But he sensed that something was amiss, and demanded to know what it was.

In that exact moment when their eyes met, Sejal had picked up her axe. It was her favourite weapon, and she always kept it by her side. She had had it since she was 9. Her action was mechanical. She had no intention of bringing it down on him but from where Rana was seeing it, he probably felt that it could have struck him, or worse, that it was meant to strike him. Caught off guard, Sejal rushed out of the shed, and plunged into the night.

She staggered down the hill and away from the den where they had been holed up that month. They were somewhere in Rechela Danda, the highest point in the Neora Valley in the Kalimpong Hills in Darjeeling. On a good day, they could see Mount Kanchenjunga from where they stood. The forest was plush with rhododendrons, bamboo, ferns, oak, sal and orchids. It was also home to clouded leopards, red panda and musk deer. But for the most part, it was heaven, in spite of the danger of being there!

They had had such a wonderful time there, he and she—hunting, trudging through the forest, honing their skills and being madly in love. Now and then, they would plunder a village and make away with the loot. They got by. And then, the time would come for another attack. This routine went on for eight years before something broke. Sejal had no idea that this was coming. Rana was oblivious.

They had just pulled off a remarkable heist and were biding their time until the coast cleared. This had been one of their largest gambles, and a heady adventure for her. She was a trainee, poised to graduate soon. She was able to take independent decisions, though, and was not afraid of the consequences. Even before they had set out on this job, it had been decided that they would remain on the sidelines until things simmered down.

And here she was, running away from someone she had passionately loved only weeks ago. How things could go from completely normal to quite unsalvageable in a matter of just a few months, she couldn't fathom. Perhaps the split happened in one precise moment, and the realization came much later! She couldn't put a finger on it, not yet!

The former lovers raced through a patch which was the most thickset of the region. Sejal was tired from carrying the axe but she wasn't going to throw it away. It gave her strength, and it would come in handy with wild animals.

It was a difficult flight. She was frail but determined. She didn't want to be caught by her beloved. All she had wanted, in the recent past, was to be with him, care for him and love him. But that feeling had died. She may have stopped loving him. Maybe the crime got to her. Or worse, she could've been bored.

As she kept fleeing him, Sejal tried to recall that initial

attraction. They had just found one another, one day, many years ago. She was young and bold. He was a savage; large, uncouth and coarse. She was short, half his size, average-looking, and burnt from being in the sun. She had run away from home, having decided that life as a farmer's daughter was not meant for her. She was only 18. Rana liked wild cats.

When they first met, she often provoked and challenged him. He liked that. He chose her to be his partner. He was a notorious criminal, a bachelor. It was generally believed that he would stay that way. Sejal may have spoilt him and made him vulnerable. But she didn't care. She had an idyllic time with him and she was not going to change that.

She had fallen for his masculinity, that ruggedness, that daring. When Rana first found her, she had been hiding in the forest. A young girl, all alone, and fast asleep. It had been two months since she had left her home in the hills one clammy night. Thereafter, it had been a lot of running and hiding, and then, some more of that. Sejal did not have a plan.

When she woke up, she found herself in his hideout, on a bale of hay, with a rug thrown over her body. She was relieved to have been rescued. The fact that Rana was a miscreant did not bother her. He was nearly thirty but she treated him like a peer. She talked to him and he listened.

She practised the art of picking locks. Rana also taught

her how to use a knife. Sejal was getting better with the gun, too. His wolf pack was a sizeable one; all-male. No one misbehaved with her although there had been one attempt during the initial phase. But after it was handled with an iron hand, everyone got the message. The pocket edition was the chief's mistress.

She sprinted every morning. She liked the rush of adrenaline during that run. He encouraged her. With time, she was moving faster than he was. She had also been trained to ride a horse and was becoming quite the ideal bandit herself. It wasn't a bad life; most certainly more interesting than her erstwhile staid routine. She felt no remorse for having made this choice. She did not miss the family and she never wanted to return to them. All she wanted was to spend her life with that gentle rogue and be loved and cherished by him.

But one fateful event must have changed something between them. One night, as they lay in each other's arms, spent and intoxicated, he said, "Just another five years of all this and then we must do something else. Do you have any ideas?" Rana had often spoken about going away to Bhutan and starting a business there. It was a wake-up call. Sejal did want to be with this man but was she planning to be with him forever? She was twenty-six. It had already been eight years.

She wasn't sure. She was still very wild. She wanted to explore life; explore other men. She didn't want her story to end typically—lover, wife, mother, ennui! Settling down would mean pots and the pans; and tiny tots. That was not the future Sejal wanted. She was far too adventurous and risqué for that.

Her body language may have started changing on that night. She couldn't sense it then but hurtling down that mountain now, she could see it clearly. She remained the lover but a part of her had perhaps begun planning an exit. She liked him. That was a great life. But she wanted more.

The bandits were to carry out a major heist at that point. That distracted Sejal from herself for a while. Elaborate plans had been chalked out for a foolproof operation. The gang normally raided villages far away from the hideout just before the break of dawn and sprayed sleeping gas to keep the occupants unconscious. Sejal worked on the locks and on the safe. There was no bloodshed. They crept in skillfully and left without a sound.

But on that night, she was distracted. It took her longer than usual to undo the locks. Rana had begun getting agitated. The safe had been well-hidden. They had lost precious time. When it was finally traced in the kitchen, deep in the ground, Sejal got to work. She left no trace at the scene of crime. And yet, Rana and she both knew that something was amiss. Sure enough, one of family members woke up at the last minute, and pounced upon them with a rifle.

Sejal managed to slip out of the place, hopped on her mare and made her escape. Many gang members were galloping by her side. But Rana wasn't among them. In all his thirteen years as a thief, he had never once been caught. The gang made it to the hideout after six hours, carrying enough moolah. But their chief was missing in action. "Did you see him come out?" his right hand man asked Sejal. She kept quiet. She had abandoned her partner in a jiffy. Perhaps he was hurt, or worse, he could have been shot.

"I'm going back," said the scruffy man, as he gave her a dirty look, and left to look for his chief. Sejal knew that she should've used that opportunity. She had the money, the courage, and a plan. She could have run away to Sikkim and then, moved further away. But she didn't. Around dawn, she heard some shuffling. Rana had returned. He had been shot but he had escaped. Her heart went out to him.

But 'each one for himself' was the mantra of the tribe, and she had only done what she had been trained to do. But this heist had been a bust. The police would be at their heels soon. Rana held a meeting with the gang and ordered everyone to move. All twenty-two members made haste. They knew where and when they were supposed to congregate. Sejal knew that they had to move quickly as well, or they'd be caught.

"Why aren't we going along?" she asked him gently. He did not respond. He looked at her suspiciously, as if she had left him behind, on purpose. "Get some rest. We'll leave early tomorrow morning," he said. He was terse, cold. She tried to fuss over him. He pushed her way. He had withdrawn. Something had soured. Sejal decided to make her move. She was going to leave him. And that is how she had charged out of their hideout, and plunged into the night.

Stumbling past trees and bushes, she ran on. Her legs ached and she felt that she would collapse. But taking a break wasn't an option. He would catch up with her. So, she kept going on. She had fallen several times on the way, and had begun to bleed from her left leg. She had bruises and cuts from being sheared by thorns. She had also rammed into a large boulder and that had left a deep gash on her temple.

Even if she could out-run him, Sejal knew that she wouldn't survive for too long if she didn't take a break. It had been more than an hour and a half and both of them had still been running when she heard a loud cry. The forest was still. Rana had taken a severe fall, or worse, he had been attacked. Must she reach out to him or continue on her journey?

Sejal stood transfixed, weary and bleeding, and trying to decide. If she went back, her chance at a new life would be over. She ought to run away. Then, she heard him call out her name. It was one, hoarse cry, and then deathly silence. He needed her. He was seriously injured. In any case, he had been shot only a few hours ago. She broke off a large, strong branch, and using it as a crutch, began trudging uphill. It was going to be a tedious climb.

The minutes grew longer and more tiresome. Dawn was about to break. There would be some light soon. She could hear his breathing now. She was close. She pushed off the last set of leaves blocking her view. It was a gruesome sight. He must have plunged off or toppled over a rock. Rana had landed face down right on top of a sharp, thick tree stub. It had pierced his body right through the stomach. He had collapsed and was bleeding away to death.

With whatever was left of him, he acknowledged her presence. There was no expression save that of severe pain in his eyes. Blood gushed out of his mouth and from the wound on his arm. Sejal knew that she had to help him but trying to pull him out would mean sure death. The stub had sheared a hole, the size of a football, in him. He would be gone in seconds. So, she sat by him and put her hand to her heart. She began crying. She sought his forgiveness.

"I'm sorry. I don't know what came over me. I made a mistake. Trust me!" she said. He was losing consciousness. She couldn't bear to see him suffer like that. She had loved him for so long. He looked at her axe. She understood what he was trying to convey. "No! But I cannot do that. I cannot," she whimpered. Rana beseeched her. His pain was unbearable. So, with a broken heart, torn and wounded, Sejal brought her weapon into position, and with one final resolve, let it fall over his neck; a guillotine. And, he was gone.

****

Muchchad Gadh

Professor Lyndoh, who taught me History in college, has been on an interesting journey across the country for a while now. I got a letter recently, from somewhere in Rajasthan. Here is how it goes:-

Dear Sangita,

I'm in a quaint little village in south-west Rajasthan, somewhere between Barmer and Jalore, where everyone sports a moustache, except the women and the children, of course. It is called Muchchad Gadh. To be honest, some of the women here have moustaches too...faint, feeble ones... unlike their male counterparts. The men boast of the more handsome variety of this predominantly male accessory. No one who has lived in this village has ever shaved the moustache away; it is against custom.

Moreover, it is uncommon to find small, puny samples. These moustaches are reared like crop, and groomed with great care and devotion. Therefore, they grow long and thick, and beam with fiery, desert pride. Isn't it intriguing that those who live in the grip of the heat do not want to do away with so much facial hair? These and other such questions had bugged me. The only way to find out more was to go to ground zero and investigate for oneself.

So, one day, after I had put in the required amount of time on the research, background et al, I decided to hit the road for some field experience. I packed my bags, and left for Moustache Village. It was a long trip. I did not know how they would react to me. I am as clean shaven as a new born baby. But I had no intention of returning without finishing my study. I was going to stay there for a month, no matter what. I wondered what I would say…and how I would undertake the project. It isn't easy just walking into someone's life and expecting them to embrace you. One needed to put in the requisite time and effort.

I was dropped somewhere near the village, and directed to walk for a "little while" to my right. Before I could ask anything else, the rickety, green-coloured bus with not a single window pane in place, and suffering from severe wear and tear, rattled away on its journey. I was left wondering if I had heard the conductor right. I had tried to talk to him a bit during the trip but he was uneasy and shifty-eyed; he kept looking away from me, and the radio was playing very loud music. "So, *'you'* are going to Muchchad Gadh," he said repeatedly with a lot of emphasis on the 'you'… as if it was a crime for someone without a moustache to go there!

I began dragging my feet over the sand, carrying my large, sturdy backpack. It had travelled the world with me; and without it, I felt rather stripped. The "little" turned out to be an eight kilometer trudge, with the sun burning down on me at 49 degrees. It must have been an insane moment when I had decided to indulge in such folly. But worse has been done in the past. Much has been suffered. Therefore, this was going to be one more sojourn. I finally began seeing the outlines of a village.

The children were the first ones to spot me. Some ran towards me; others ran to their elders. Soon, several people lined up to size this unexpected visitor. As I inched closer, I could see the consternation in the crowd. People put their mouths to ears. I was fairly close to them. When I took off my cap along with the cloth that covered my face, there was a palpable gasp from the audience. Was something wrong? Did I look hideous? I hadn't thought about the fact that I did not look like them at all. I did not have a moustache and I had never had a beard, or so, I think!

A tall man, nearly 6'3", wearing a traditional dhoti, a

dusty white kurta and a brown waistcoat, approached me. His turban was a flaming red-orange, and it stood out starkly against the sand. The *mojaris* on his feet were exquisitely crafted, and he carried a thick, ornate stick made of camel bone. He had exceptionally limpid, grey eyes, which bore down at me. I learnt that he was the village chief, Surja Mal Bangad.

"Who are you and what is the purpose of your visit?" he probed. The boom in his voice affected me. There was so much bass in it. I shuffled a bit, and put my bag down. I was tired. "I'm a research scholar," I began. He waited for me to continue. I don't know whether he was getting the drift. He seemed so stoic and uninfluenced. He cocked his head to the left and looked at me purposefully.

"I am a professor from a college in Jodhpur," was my second line. He nodded. "So, you are a teacher?" he asked. I bobbed my head up and down.

"He teaches children," he shouted out to his people. There was some nodding and jostling in the crowd. Bangad relaxed and waited for me to go on. "I am extremely curious about your village," I said. He looked at me as if that was no explanation at all. Perhaps it wasn't. So, I tried again.

"I have come to know about something very unique in this village. And, I am eager to find out as to why every adult male here sports a moustache despite all this heat," I stated in my best voice. It had been modulated to sound completely non-threatening and humble. Bangad was supremely amused. His teeth were visible as he broke into a generous smile. So, I continued with the rest of my prelude. "I'd like to stay here for a month and carry out my research," I said. He played with his beard.

He made a gesture with his hands which meant I was supposed to go away and give him a little space. Meanwhile, the elders of the village crowded up to him. They had several questions to ask. "Who is this stranger? Why a sudden visit to our village? We don't like intrusions. Suggest another village. Who knows how he'll behave. Send him on his way," they urged.

They were told about my research about a region where moustaches ruled the roost, and where baby-faced adults or those without these symbols of manhood were unwelcome. As if to indicate what he thought about me, a steely male, who had the longest moustache in Muchchad Gadh, twirled it, as he sized me up. I gave him my most amicable expression—part Gandhara Buddha, part Anavyssos Kouros; part Avalokiteswara, part Achilles.

I would find out over the next few days that Karni Raj Palgota, whose prized moustache was twelve feet long, was a celebrity in that village; having won the Mr Desert Tournament that takes place in Jaisalmer, every February, during the Desert Festival, six times in a row. He was forty, and it had taken him over 20 years to scale this peak. His *crop* had been nurtured with almond oil, curd, ghee and lemon every day for over two decades now.

Bangad ordered his people to lead me into the shade. They offered me a glass of water—a prized commodity in the desert land, and beckoned me to put myself down on a cot. He congregated with the seniors; looking at me repeatedly and with some amount of intrigue. Time went by. The children looked at me as if I was an exotic creature. One of them, a thin boy, about eight or nine, came up to me, and tried to touch my hair, which was spiky and short from a recent haircut.

The women of the village, covered from top to toe in a riot of colour, peeped at me from behind their striking veils. What could they be thinking? I looked at their long, flowing skirts, open back *kanchlis* (blouses) and bright, shining *odhnis* (long scarfs) with admiration. They wore a lot of ivory bangles and sported various kinds of traditional tattoos. They were carefully examining my muddy green dungarees and plain black t-shirt.

A senior citizen caught my gaze, and I looked away. I wasn't supposed to stare at these gorgeous women. They were absolutely regal, tall and sturdy and naturally stunning. They wore no make-up and had none of the airs that their peers in modern cities had. Yet, they had no match when it came to organic beauty. None. I got up from the comfort of the cot, wondering what would ensue, when Bangad came out of the meeting.

"Alright! You can stay here with us. But that will be under strict supervision," he announced. "You will keep me informed about all your activities," he warned me. "You will not meet anyone unless I give you permission to do so," he said very severely. I immediately nodded. "You will respect our customs and traditions," he stressed. "And, finally, before you write anything, you will have to get that cleared by us," he declared.

"If this is acceptable to you, you can stay on. Otherwise, you can leave as soon as you have had something to eat," he pronounced. Of course, I accepted. I wanted so intensely to be around these incredible people, and observe their way of life. There was no way I was going to compromise my situation by crossing the line. I was going to be good and I would do exactly as was told.

So, my journey with this tribe began. It was among the most fascinating ones I've had in all my life. Slowly and gradually, I found out that the main occupation of these people was making *mojaris* (leather shoes) and carved wooden furniture. I traveled with them and met the *Bhopas* (priest singers) and the *Dholis* (drummers) in the area. I also met the *Rebaris*, who are camel and sheep breeders, and who work with camel skin. They make stunning handicraft items, and they gifted me a camel skin water bag, which I now carry with me.

Life in this village was not too predictable although there were some picture post card scenarios. Women painting and decorating the mud walls of their huts with motifs of trees, leaves, flowers, birds and animals, and gods and goddesses. When this happened, the sandy walls came alive with colour—red, green, blue, yellow, pink and black. Beejli and Banwri, two sisters, who were experts at making these colours from vegetable dyes, shared them with the other women.

Every evening, between four and five, the men congregated at the *chaupal,* the village square. I was put up in a room at the local school, which was right next to it. So, I got a great view of these social gatherings.

What was most fascinating was the '*Moocha Ri*' ceremony that took place every week, without fail. Professionals massaged several moustaches with mustard oil and pressed them into shape by tying a cloth around the faces of the men.

Limba Ram, the Mooch Maker, was quite in demand during these times. He rode a large black motorcycle that made a lot of noise when it approached the *chaupal.* He was quite well-off and this was not his vocation; styling moustaches was just his passion. He had styled several moustaches, he told me. I wonder how he did that.

There was quite a variety. There was the Hungarian style moustache—big and bushy, and quite popular. One or two men in the village even sported the Dali kind of moustache—thin, long and narrow, and curved steeply upward. There were many Imperial Moustaches—with whiskers growing from the upper lip and the cheeks, and curled upward, meticulously.

When the men saw me looking at them intently, they would invite me to the *chaupal.* I often heard comments such as, 'A man without a moustache is like a cup of tea without sugar'. I was quite fine with sugar free tea. "C'mon, haven't you ever felt like growing one?" I was often asked. They saw my expression and laughed out loud. Dungar Punia, one of the older men of the village, would come to my rescue, just out of courtesy, and when he had me in his clutches, would tease me softly. His was a Walrus moustache; bushy, and covering his entire mouth.

After their moustaches had been groomed, there would be song and dance. I was often dragged to centre stage, and I obliged, although a bit shyly. Trying to follow their graceful, lithe movements made me feel liberated. And by and by, I began looking forward to these sessions.

I was given an orange turban as a gift; a sign of happiness. The younger of the men wore red turbans that were symbols of love. I wonder why I didn't get one of those. It wasn't as if I was going to take advantage of the situation and fall for someone. Or was that a possibility? Who knows? Could something untoward and exciting happen to me? Or, was I going to be treated with compassion and regard, and nothing more?

The time for my departure is now on the anvil. One of these days, I hope to get Bangad's clearance on the piece I have written on his people and their lifestyle. He does not read English and has, therefore, asked to me write the piece in Hindi, which I have done. He has been generous to a fault. He has looked after me and given me more than my share. He has spoken to me at length despite his reservations about visitors, and shared a part of his story with me, thereby helping me understand this region and these people, better.

When I put this series together later this year, I will be able to tell the world about the fascinating people of this desert state, who bowled me over with their hospitality, their warmth and their concern for my well-being. I might even look forward to getting a few letters from some of them.

And, I, who has never had a moustache in all these years, now sport a fine, young one. It will take a little getting used to…but not for one second have I regretted this decision.

Besides, I believe I am now going to be connected to this village for life. You see, despite Bangad's supervision and in spite of his embargo on me, Beejli and I have fallen in love, I think.

How did that happen? Well, first, the eyes met. Then, they spoke. Saying things you could only, at first, say in your head. Then, the eyes received. They were startled. But pleasantly so. Then, there was the odd beckoning. The eyes beckoned. They dared to do so. They questioned. They pushed the eyebrows up to do so. They glanced quickly. They were forlorn. They showed excitement. They twinkled.

And, during the dance in the *chaupal*, they made commitments that no one else was aware of. I believe I am going to marry her. She seems amenable to the idea of going away with me. We've had a chat. I shall also soon have to break the news to Bangad and to all the men and the women in the village. After all, I'm going to be their relative very soon. And, how could any son-in-law of Muchhad Gadh not have a 'moustache' to boast of?

Best Wishes to you. Write to me soon.

Dong Thau Lyndoh.

****

The Time Has Come

"I don't care how you manage it but I want you home on Friday," said the senior Mrs Chatterjee to her eldest son. And although he was thirty-five, he still felt compelled to accede to his mother's demands. He nodded his head feebly without committing anything yet. Shonin Chatterjee worked as the marketing head of a pharmaceutical giant in Bhopal in central India. Its factories and labs were in the city, and the company had a reasonably effective distribution network across the country.

How on earth could he manage to stay back home on a week day, he wondered as he picked up his bag and the car keys? His mother was demanding and pushy, as mothers can sometimes be. She had done this to him in the past, as well. He had no choice but to give in to the pressure for the sake of peace at home. When he stood up to her commands, he had to pay for months. There would be snide one-liners and underhand remarks.

His wife, meek and timid, would have to suffer some discomfort as well—the murmurs at the dining table and the drone on Sunday mornings. But she shared a decent rapport with her mother-in-law, and the women could suddenly gang up, without warning. "Please listen to your mother. It is for your own sake. Why are you being so stubborn?" she asked him softly.

Why was his being at a *puja* so important? Agreed that the prayers were being held for him… but they could be performed without his presence! "This *yajna* is being held for your safety, for your life," his mother had said, her eyes wide, and the expression in them, insistent. "Don't you remember punditji looking at your *janampatri* last week and making that announcement?" she gritted. Shonin couldn't care for such humbug. But he didn't say that to his mother.

How could an astrologer foretell his future when the creature had no inkling about what would happen to him, in the first place? Did predictions matter? Did they not feed on insecurities and baseless beliefs? Shonin was a man of reason and did not encourage conjecture. It seemed absurd to suggest to him that he was going to die in exactly three weeks!

All hell had broken loose when this catastrophe hit the Chatterjee household. Mrs Chatterjee had been to her friend, Uma Bhanot's place, and had encountered an astrologer there. "Punditji has been advising our family for over a decade now. He is always right. And, because of his interventions, we've avoided bad luck several times," said Mrs Bhanot, trying to influence her friend. But Sarla Chatterjee needed no convincing. She was already on board.

She made an appointment with Pundit Ram Vilochan Bharadwaj to pay her a visit over the weekend, and he had landed with alacrity. Once she got the formalities out of the way, Mrs Chatterjee brought out the horoscopes of her children and grand-children. Her other sons also lived in the city, and were equally well-placed. Pundit Bharadwaj took his time, using his paraphernalia, to do his job, and then looked sharply at his hostess.

"I don't know how to say this to you but something inauspicious in on the anvil. Should I share this with you? Are you ready to hear it?" he asked. Sarla's muscles contracted and the veins on her neck stood up. "What is it, punditji?" she asked, visibly nervous. "Is it that bad?"

The astrologer kept a deadpan expression for a second and then made the announcement, "There will be a death in the family, very soon," he said. Sarla put her hand to her mouth. She was shocked. She thought about herself and about her husband; both were advancing in years. "What do you see, punditji? Please tell me quickly. The anxiety is killing me already," she said.

The astrologer adjusted his stance; looked a bit reluctant and then, opened his mouth. "Your eldest son will die a month from now," he announced. You can imagine what a mother would go through on hearing such news. Sarla Chatterjee recoiled from the man; looked about herself and then did what she was instinctively used to doing. She rushed to her husband.

Amitosh Chatterjee had retired from the Income Tax Department. He was a soft-spoken, simple man, who despised noise and quibble. He couldn't get into tangles with his better half. He surrendered to her whims. He was sitting in his sanctum, scanning the newspapers of the day. He saw his wife in tears and asked, "What happened, Sarla?" She did not respond. "What happened? Say something," he pushed.

"I cannot even repeat what I have just heard. You have to come out with me and talk to him," she blabbered incoherently. "But who is this and what is he saying?" asked Amitosh, quite befuddled.

"Have you forgotten? Pundit Bharadwaj is here and he is saying awful things. Talk to him. Ask him again. What will we do now? My poor Shonin," she wailed. Amitosh Chatterjee pulled himself out of the comfort of his easy chair and walked to the living room.

A man sat there on one of the chairs, dressed in a white *kurta* and *dhoti*. He had the typical orange cloth that pundits wear, thrown around his shoulders. His forehead was smeared with vermillion and sandalwood paste. And, he was checking messages on his cell phone. "*Namaskar*," said Amitosh Chatterjee. "My wife seems to be completely distraught by whatever it is that you have told her. What is the matter?" he enquired.

The doomsayer remained seated calmly, sans emotion on his face. "I'm terribly sorry, Mr Chatterjee, but there is very bad news for the family," he began. Amitosh leaned towards the man, in anticipation. "Yes. What is it?" he asked. "It is very difficult for me to share this with you but I cannot change what the future holds. Can I?" he offered, apologetically.

Amitosh Chatterjee was getting impatient, nervous, scared. "Please just say it and relieve me of my anxiety," he pleaded. "Mr Chatterjee, according to this horoscope…and I believe it is of your eldest child…the time ahead is tragic," said the astrologer, prolonging the older man's misery.

"Yes. What does it say?" asked the shaken father.

"If indeed this is his horoscope, your son will be dead

in a month's time," the astrologer declared.

Amitosh Chatterjee felt his heart miss a beat. "What do you mean? He is absolutely healthy. How could anything happen to him?" he stressed. "I cannot tell you what will go wrong. But his horoscope shows that this person will not live beyond this month," offered the pundit.

"You must be out of your mind. Have you checked it properly? Maybe, the noting on the paper is all wrong. There has to be an error," Amitosh rambled.

The astrologer sat stoic, as if expecting that reaction. "I assure you, Mr Chatteree, I have read this again and again before coming to the same conclusion. Still, if you have doubts, I challenge you to show it around. I don't think there will be any change," he said. Amitosh Chatterjee had lost his sense of balance. Moreover, to see this sort of arrogance irked him.

"Thank you for your reading. But you can leave now," said Amitosh. "Here is your fee. I hope I never see you again," he added quietly, rushing at the astrologer, and nearly herding him out of the house.

"What are you doing?" protested his wife. "I'm so sorry, punditji. Please stay back and tell us what to do," she pleaded. "My husband obviously does not want to take this seriously but I do," she added. But the astrologer had been put off my Amitosh's impunity. "I must leave right now. Call me again later," he said curtly, pocketed his fee, and left in a rush.

"Look what you have done," wailed Sarla. "We should have at least found out how to avoid this calamity," she said. Collapsing on the sofa in the living room, she began crying her heart out. Her husband, as most men of that breed, found himself cornered. He went up to her gingerly and tried to calm her down.

"Aren't you being a little silly, Sarla? Someone turns up and announces something like this and you are willing to believe it right away?" he quizzed. Sarla made a face at him. She was very annoyed.

"And, why do you insist on seeing astrologers?" her husband asked. "Don't you know better than to pursue such things?" he said, sternly. It wasn't having the desired effect on his spouse. Nevertheless, he tried one more time. "Now, collect yourself and forget about this. All will be well," he counseled. Sarla gave her head a violent half shake. All was not going to be well. Meanwhile, the elderly couple had not noticed that Shonin's wife, Nilanjana, had heard everything, and that she had fainted in the kitchen.

"Oh Ma… Nilu," cried out Mrs Chatterjee. She sprinkled a little water on the young woman's face, and tried to revive her. "Now look, the bad times have already begun. Has Nilu ever fainted before? You shouldn't have thrown out punditji like that. Now, who will help us? Why did I have to be married to a non-believer? I wish my brothers were here right now. They would have understood my trauma. You never understood me in all these forty years. How I have wasted my life with you?" Sarla Chatterjee exploded. She had clearly lost it.

Amitosh ignored his wife and tried to focus on his daughter-in-law. She was so frail. Once she had recovered, Nilu, too, couldn't help but talk about the prophecy. "Ma, what will happen now? This is unbearable. What am I to do? *Ma Durga*, help me tide over this crisis! Bless this household! Bless my husband! Don't take him away from me. What error have I committed? Please punish me, Ma, don't punish him," she sobbed.

'Come, come, my dear. Calm down. Don't take the words of astrologers too seriously. Nothing will happen to Shonin," assured Amitosh Chatterjee, part disbelieving himself and not knowing what to do. Everyone was disconsolate, shaken up and at a loss for solutions. 'Must I believe this?' thought Amitosh. 'I will have to get another pundit into the picture and resolve this,' thought Sarla. And Nilanjana continued to pray fervently, and with great devotion. She couldn't bear to think of life without Shonin. He was a good man.

When he returned from work that night, she divulged

everything to him although it was difficult for her to get the words out. Shonin was amused. "What is this I hear?" he asked his parents, at dinner. No one was forthcoming. They looked sombre. How could one even discuss such a delicate matter? "Why do you even go to astrologers, in any case, Ma?" he asked his mother. Within the next twenty-four hours, his younger brothers, their wives and some other relatives had been told of this episode.

There was a deluge of suggestions. The believers advised Sarla to definitely take remedial measures. There were invitations to trips to various parts of the country to see even more celebrated astrologers. There was a lot of sighing and disbelief and the customary display of empathy and there was the odd casting off of such baloney. "You must take a second opinion," advised her elder sister, who also lived in Bhopal. "I'll refer my astrologer to you," she added.

So, Sarla Chatterjee showed that particular horoscope to the second astrologer. The outcome was the same. But Pundit Madan Chaturvedi asked her to get a huge sacrificial prayer (*yagna*) performed to avert the disaster. "There is always a remedy, sister," he assured. "The ceremony is a bit elaborate and will cost you but it will help your son survive. And, obviously, he will have to be present during the entire time," he stressed. Therefore, Sarla wanted her son to be present for the occasion.

The neighbours had been invited to participate in the 'welfare prayers'. Relatives were to pour in. On D Day, the house was full of unruly smoke and the fragrance of burning incense sticks. Wishes were to be sent up, heavenward. Four pundits, led by their chief, threw a lot of stuff into the holy fire, and chanted mantras. Shonin had to take the first half of the day off and put up with every ritual. At the end of three hours, the pundits declared that all was well now. And, Shonin left for work, quite irritated.

By the time the next week dawned upon the household, Sarla Chatterjee had arranged for a driver to take her eldest child to office. "This is just a temporary measure. Once the fateful day passes us by, I will let you drive," she told her son. Meanwhile, she kept in touch with Pundit Chaturvedi and kept getting tips from him. Shonin was forced to wear amulets and stones for protection. His mother also tried to smear his forehead with ash one morning as he was leaving for work. "There is no shame in this," she said, as he protested. "Is there any shame in being religious?" she asked, as he wiped it off.

Things were getting quite unmanageable for Shonin. His peers and staff wondered why he was wearing several red and yellow threads on his right wrist; why he looked distracted and as to why his mother had begun calling him ten times at work. It was usually the same question. "Are you okay?" Could one blame her for being so concerned? She also sent several figurines of Gods and Goddesses to his office and asked his assistant to discreetly keep them on his table. Not many Indians would find it in themselves to remove them.

At home, everyone was reciting the *Mahamrityunjay Mantra* to keep death at bay. And then, as luck would have it, Shonin's car was involved in an accident. It wasn't the driver's fault. They were returning late at night from an official dinner at a local hotel. The company's Bulgarian partners were being wined and dined on their annual visit to the country. Shonin's car was at 90 kms per hour. Suddenly, a larger, much sturdier vehicle jumped the red light and rammed into his car from the right side at a T angle. Both Shonin and the driver suffered concussions and bruises; the windscreen had cracked up, and the shards had cut them, too. The erring driver had abandoned his vehicle and run away.

There was complete mayhem at the Chatterjee household. "Didn't I tell you that you must take these predictions seriously?" chided Sarla. "But Ma, we were not at fault. The other car jumped a light," protested Shonin. "Still, you could have lost your life. Thank God you were not driving. Who knows what would have happened then. You drive even faster," his mother responded. After that, she wasn't sure whether even the driver could protect her son.

The incident rattled Shonin a bit. What if the pundit's forecast was right, he thought, for the first time. He discussed the matter with the younger of his two siblings, whom he was close to. Dwaipayan was a sensible, calm man, who took enough time to ponder over matters before reacting to them. His was an approach of restraint and reserve. "Shonin, no harm being a little cautious," he said. "We don't have to let this drive us into a tizzy, though," he added. He also contacted Pundit Chaturvedi and had a few chats with him.

But Sarla Chatterjee was not in a mood to let go of caution. When it came to the last week, she ordered her son, "You will not leave this house all week." He resisted with all his might and got an interjection. "That's absurd, Ma. I cannot be away from work all week," he protested. "Are you still hung up on what was said? Please don't worry. Nothing will happen to me," he assured his harassed mother. D Day was to fall on Friday. "But on Thursday, I will not let you leave," she shot back. Her son shrugged that off and left the area.

On Wednesday, his mother took ill. It must have been the strain. Perforce, he had to pitch in. He called in sick. Each time he tried to leave the house, he got a sob story. It was imperative that he be at work. But he couldn't leave all day. Come Thursday, his mother's condition deteriorated. She had high fever and was delirious. Once again, Shonin had to stay home.

On Friday, he got dressed for work. Word got to his mother and she called out for him. "You will leave this house over my dead body," she warned him.

"Ma, I've already missed two days of work. There are deadlines and presentations, and I must be there," he pleaded. But she would not relent. She cried till her eyes were red and swollen. In the past, whenever she had taken ill, Nilanjana would look after her but now she wanted Shonin around. His brothers offered to help but the mother stubbornly refused.

All day went by and Shonin began feeling caged. The phone rang consistently. He could not confide in his bosses lest they take him for a lunatic. He attended to e-mails and pending blue prints but a crucial meeting was on and he felt guilty for skipping that. By evening, he would've strangled someone. He had nothing pleasant to say to his wife. At dinner, he was completely withdrawn.

D day had almost passed him by. His father was resilient. His mother was nervous, and had been reciting mantras all day. Nilanjana had spent most of her time in the small shrine in the house. Everyone was waiting for the sun to set upon this unwelcome episode when Dwaipayan came calling, with Pundit Chaturvedi in tow. "It is important to keep reciting the mantra to keep the situation under control," said the astrologer.

All attention was immediately focused on him. "Have you been reciting the mantra yourself?" the pundit asked Shonin. He had not done that. "This is not good. You should have done that," remarked the pundit. Angry, irritated and enervated, Shonin stepped out to the balcony for some fresh air. Lighting up a cigarette, he looked at the houses on the other side of the road. His neighbours on the floor above his had laid out their clothes to dry and a saree kept flying at his face. It was windy.

'I feel like a fool,' he thought. 'Why…Oh why did I give in to this absurdity?' he asked himself repeatedly. It was even more embarrassing that some of his office staff had come home to have some papers signed and heard his mother talking loudly on the phone. She seemed absolutely fine. In any case, who misses a meeting when there's help at home, and when it is not an emergency?

'I'm never going to listen to this stuff again,' thought Shonin. The astrologer joined him on the balcony. "The day is almost gone. It is just a matter of a few hours," he assured him. Shonin looked uneasy. He could not ask the pundits of the world to go to hell and he did not have the conviction to follow what they asked him to do. He pulled hard at the saree which had flown into his face for the tenth time, meaning to get it off the string, in uncontrollable anger. Punditji stepped forward to help him out. A brick which had kept the cloth from flying away came crashing upon the pundit with the last violent tug and hit him hard on the head. He died instantly.

****

Oshbo

He was twenty-nine. He stood at 5'1". He had the calculative acumen of a 45-year-old and the shrewdness of a hyena-jackal hybrid. He worked for a newspaper, and was keen to become the country's hottest investigative correspondent. He was a part of the organization's prized 'Expose' team, and had had considerable success. He was always at the boss's feet; by the water coolers; and in the union offices, picking up the gossip and using it as ammunition.

Oshbo spoke in muffled tones, in the manner of a spy. He was shifty-eyed and secretive, and had many unsavory stories to share. Meeting Oshbo meant collecting a gossip that you could pass on. Cabinet Ministers and their torrid affairs; the amount of land being usurped by a corporate house in a suburb or in the hinterland; the ego hassles of an Under Secretary to the Government of India; the expansion plans of a rival media house. He soaked up a lot—rumours, speculation, yarn! Nothing was sacred. Any information was welcome.

There was a catch, though. You had to return the favour, given that he was entertaining you, and bringing colour to your otherwise routine job. The failure to reciprocate was viewed with disfavor. He'd become dismissive, and in time, all you got was an obscure nod, a furtive glance or the hint of a scowl. Or, he shunned you completely. After that, the gossip came to you, pre-owned, worn and stale.

Oshbo was in office all the time. He was the first one to arrive and always the last one to leave, other than the night reporters and the building staff, of course. He had friends there, too. He passed on gifts that he may have received during junkets and press conferences that he did not want—calendars, tacky-looking diaries and decorative bric-a-brac. He hobnobbed with labour union representatives on the one hand, and held secret meetings with sources from the bureaucracy, on the other.

He was also brazenly sycophantic. He rarely left his editor's side. He defended him against all detractors, and he protected him from the idiosyncrasies of the senior managers on the advertising side. They had clout, and could tweak the material. He had allies there, too. Perhaps he was a mole for the management, informing it of the machinations of the minions in the newsroom. Oshbo had his pulse on everything. He knew who towed the management's line. He was aware of those trying to plant stories. He knew everyone's political ideologies; their sympathies for the Left; their right wing affiliations and inclinations. He was a veritable asset.

His hold over his immediate superiors was enviable. First thing, every morning, he read half a dozen newspapers. He started early. Then, he made a dozen phone calls. His contacts plied him with ample dope, and he came sufficiently loaded to work. He knew of every little political development of the previous night, and he usually had a list of potential news stories for the day. He had no qualms about running errands for his masters. He was the coffee boy and the private secretary, as also the chief advisor.

His bureau chief, during the phase in context, was a short, fair man with penetrative eyes and long hair. He was in his 50s. He sported a thick moustache; smoked Cuban cigars, and wore flamboyant suits and ties. He disliked the paan-chewing, kurta-wearing journalist. He was irreverent, Left-leaning, and partial to sommeliers and art aficionados. He had been in London for five years before returning to Delhi.

Oshbo grew his hair long; bought himself some decent shirts, and started reading up on wine and cheese although he hated the elite and was disgusted by snobbery. He was a small town chap with raw enthusiasm for everything desi and indigenously grown. Foreign imports didn't go down well with him. Therefore, for the most part during conversations with the bureau head, he just nodded, as if accepting everything. His senior was never the wiser. He was quite relieved to find a lackey. The older man dragged him to fancy dinners in expensive restaurants, and he complained a lot.

"The Brie they're selling here is overrated and overpriced!"

"It is, Sir. It is," retorted Oshbo.

"They should've paired it with a Chardonnay, and that Pecorino with a Valpolicella."

"Of course, Sir," said the little guy.

"The goat should have been accompanied by a Chenin Blanc, and the Feta with a Beaujolais." Oshbo couldn't care less but he always said, "Yes, Sir. That seems just about right." Have they learnt nothing yet…cribbed the senior. "Give me a Gouda with the Merlot and a Sauvignon Blanc with my Gruyere!"

This world was alien to Oshbo. But he faked it brilliantly, and got away with it, too. He had an incredible memory, and he had learnt everything by rote. The joke that went around those days was that Oshbo would need about fifteen minutes to consult his pocket notes. If not, he couldn't take questions on food and culture. "Hey! Oshbo! I'm going to have lamb (Rogan Josh) for dinner tonight. What should I drink with it? Old Monk or Director's Special?"

He shrugged. He was terse. It depended on his mood. But he weathered the ribbing quite deftly. His ability to cope was incomparable. At times, of course, he retaliated sharply. More than the mocking per se, he was concerned about preserving his equation with his chief. None of this banter was allowed to reach the chief's office. Oshbo ensured that the man stayed insulated, and perfectly unaware of the babble outside his cabin.

One day, something changed. There was a new arrival in the bureau and to the 'Expose' team. Twenty-six-year-old Luna Huq's father had been India's cultural attache' to Belgium, and had returned to Delhi after a long stint. She had been abroad for nearly fifteen years. She spoke Dutch, French and German, and had a Masters in International Relations from Kingston University, London. She had worked briefly for *The Guardian*, and she was to cover international affairs for the newspaper.

Oshbo's boss fell hammer and tongs for the newbie.

They began taking lunch breaks together. They would go out to the corridor to smoke. One could hear the older man's booming laughter at her quips. He accompanied her to cultural evenings at the embassy. Wine tastings, art exhibitions, plays and dance recitals. Over the course of the next eight months, they had become a couple. There was enough curiosity about whether they were also sexually involved, age difference be damned!

Oshbo hated her. He thought she was being feted out of turn, and didn't quite have faith in her news-gathering abilities. He waited for her to make a mistake. But Luna was covering an area that didn't trip her up at all. It was sanitized and unhurried. Stories didn't 'break' overnight, and if they did, they could be 'analyzed' comprehensively, the following day. They didn't need to be pursued with palaver. The External Affairs Ministry held regular, genteel briefings, where accredited correspondents were invited exclusively, and in-depth discussions were possible.

Besides, she wrote well, and had an impressive knowledge base. She was iconoclastic and heretical, and always provocative. Her take on the declaration of an Islamic Caliphate by ISIS (Islamic State of Iraq and Syria); the Ebola outbreak in West Africa; the pitiable condition of the markets in Greece; her critique on the reasons for the recession in Italy; her argument against Scotland's decision to remain a part of the United Kingdom; her vitriolic piece on the Ukraine and Crimean crisis and her denouncement of the Taliban militant attack on an Army-run school in Peshawar, Pakistan, were all controversial. It was obvious that she had range, expertise and talent, and she was adroit.

One January evening, though, the bureau was a hive of activity. There was commotion, and everyone was speaking animatedly. Two gunmen, affiliated to the Islamist terrorist organization Al-Qaeda's Yemen branch, had stormed into the offices of the French satirical weekly, Charlie Hebdo, in Paris, earlier that day, shooting and killing 12 people, including two police officers. Among the butchered were leading cartoonists, columnists and artists of the magazine, including its publisher. Eleven others had been injured. People were stunned by the slaughter. World leaders conveyed horror and shock at the brutality. Parisiens were traumatized.

At this newspaper, however, the stories for the next day's edition were coming in from across the globe. Reactions on the social media, comments from intellectuals and politicians, news reports from Paris—it was a deluge. Many senior correspondents were co-opted to deal with the pressure. Oshbo was in charge of summing up the Twitter feed and getting his political contacts to give their two bit worth. Another colleague was handling the agency stories from France. Yet another was following the reaction of the Muslim Press on the Internet, checking both the conservative and the reformist sides. This continued for three days while the siege lasted.

On the fourth day, there was commotion on the floor. The editor-in-chief of the newspaper, the bureau chief and Luna were having a slanging match. The contretemps was about an editorial that she had written in response to the assault. The headline went—"Pourquoi je ne serai jamais Charlie!" (Why I will never be Charlie!). She had taken a line that was contrary to the outpouring of world-wide grief. While she condemned the bestiality of the killing, she did not spare the satirists. Blasphemy, sacrilege, religious extremism, racism, hate speech, intolerance, fundamentalism, terrorism, the line between offensive literature and radical freedom of expression were all being discussed, threadbare.

They had taken conflicting positions. The bureau head was reluctant to dilute the piece but his opposition was clement and strained. The editor-in-chief wanted it dropped. He was neither mild nor without conviction. He thought it was just too vitriolic. Luna was trying to convey that a diametrically opposite view ought to be entertained to "unclog the mind" as she kept saying.

She insisted that it be carried ad verbum, and she

wasn't going to budge. Luna had become a star writer for the newspaper. Its circulation hadn't increased over the last two years, and it was in serious financial trouble. She had perked up its profile; generated reader interest in it, and also launched its online edition. The management got involved. The owner's son-in-law had business interests in Paris—a restaurant and a designer boutique shop on the Avenue des Champs-Élysées. He didn't want the newspaper to take a soft stand—neither against the terrorists nor against France or Charlie Hebdo.

The bureau chief made one last ditch effort. He went in for a private meeting with the owner, to his home. "I do hope you'll give me time to explain my perspective," he began guardedly. And, after an unnecessary prelude, he came to the point. "You may be thwarting the very freedom of expression for which these men died. I agree that her view is contrarian. But there should be scope for it in a newspaper such as yours that claims to be liberal." Luna had made it clear to him that if he couldn't back her up on this one, she would move on.

The owner shrugged, adjusted a turquoise blue shawl around his shoulders and took a sip of his Mulligatawny soup. He then wiped it off his bushy, silver-grey moustache, and said, "I understand. I do. But this is a serious matter. The world is aghast. And, unless we support the fanatics, we cannot let this piece go, at least not so soon. When the whole world is demonstrating its support and empathy for the victims, how can a newspaper such as ours carry such an acerbic take! Perhaps in a month or so, when moderation settles in, there could be an analysis of this sort. But not tomorrow." He was resolute and unyielding.

As a last resort, the harrowed man made a frantic call to Luna's dad, who refused to get involved. He seemed surprised by her criticism of the caricaturists, though. The cultural arrogance of the French; the problems of integration and immigration in France; its value of *laicite'* and its stringent views on secularism were issues that they had discussed in the past. But he wasn't aware that her opinion on the subject had become so shrill, particularly in light of a terror threat in Brussels and Liège in 2008, which had been thwarted, and which had affected her deeply.

The next day, the newspaper carried several front page pieces on the attacks, and an editorial. But it wasn't the one that Luna had written. A senior associate editor, posted in Washington, had quickly dished out a monograph on the matter, and that had been printed. The bureau chief was distraught. He was trying very hard to assure Luna that there had been a faux pas. "I had personally ensured that the story was carried before I left for the night," he said. Luna was unconvinced, indignant and sullen.

Oshbo was blithe. He had been waiting for this day, for a long, long time. He was fed up with the undue attention Luna had been getting, and he was furious at having been cast aside by his boss. Just as he was mulling over his strategy of a reconciliation, a memorandum was circulated in office. It said—'This is a non-agenda newspaper. Options are to be left open. Let us not take sides.'

Luna put in her papers, did not wait to be relieved, and sauntered out of the building. No goodbyes. No farewell. Very surgical. A friend of hers was planning an online news magazine. She subsequently joined that and wrote freely and with gumption. She's had at least four defamation suits slapped against her, since, and nearly went to prison, once. But that hasn't deterred her. If you look carefully, you can still read between her lines, and decode the message she tries to send to her "fans".

Back at this newspaper, there was a shuffle. The bureau got a new editor. A tall, clean-shaven, handsome bohemian, who wore khadi kurtas over his frayed jeans and had short, cropped hair. He was also renowned as a poet in Varanasi. He spoke chaste Hindi and Sanskrit, and he was fond of chewing betel leaf with areca nut and slaked lime paste—paan. He was also extremely watchful of what the owners of the paper wanted in it.

The day after the new editor joined, Oshbo walked

into office. He had cut his hair short and his moustache was gone. He was in a pair of blue jeans and a light green kurta. Taking a box out of his pocket, he asked his new boss, "How about some paan, Sir? Just got it made from Pandeyji's paan shop on the North Avenue. It is absolutely fresh." The bohemian smiled, took the betel leaf contraption and deftly deposited it in the inside corner of his left cheek. "So, tell me, what do you have for the edition?"

"I have something absolutely explosive to tell you," whispered Oshbo. The boss raised his eyebrows. "Not here, Sir! It's classified. No one…but no one…except you… must get wind of this, yet! The story is developing, and believe you me, it'll be epic when it detonates!" he offered. The editor took the bait. "Why don't we go out for a stroll," suggested the newshound. Oshbo got up to his full height and flexed his shoulders. An alpha male, about to make a conquest! They walked out—a tall man, with his head bent to catch an exclusive, and a short guy, dying to share his tale.

****

The Perfect Suicide

His name was Ullas Rai. He was a 54-year-old, petit, pot-bellied man with grey hair. He was also very sick; suffering from both acute asthma and chronic alcoholism. 'Ullas' means 'joy' in Hindi. But he was neither joyful nor joyous. In fact, he was rather morose.

This narrative is from the time he had been walking through thick, unrelenting jungles somewhere in central India over three days. Ullas had prepared well for the trek. He had enough food and water, a tent and his survival kit. Was this just an adventure in the wilderness? No! Ullas was planning to commit suicide. Plain and simple; and nothing too florid.

He felt he didn't deserve to live. He had done nothing exceptional in his life thus far and was confident that he would amount to nothing great in the future. He lacked fortitude, and suffered from intellectual and emotional ataxia. There were intermittent pangs of self-doubt, and a deep sensation of 'Welterschmerz'. The Germans have been able to understand, codify and articulate even the most amorphous of emotions quite brilliantly. This one is meant to convey 'Suffering that is derived from the inevitability of a reality that never quite matches one's expectation'.

Under these abysmal circumstances, he had asked himself several times whether he ought to kill himself. He was acutely conscious that financial ruin provoked death. Shame, guilt and instability led to it as did failure in love and life.

Ullas asked himself if his was a lost cause. Had he been weak, vulnerable and negative? Had he driven himself to despair? Was he his own greatest enemy? He had lived alone in a dingy apartment. He had no companions or close friends. No one came to clean the place. And, he had no resources. He was surviving hand to mouth.

Eventually, though, after oscillating between hope and despair for a long time, he had surrendered. He had concluded that he did not have the will to fight any more. The *gyaan*, the counseling, just about everything was humbug. He forsook reason. He gave up faith.

Ullas had argued that he had waited and hoped for

twenty years for something phenomenal to happen to him. It hadn't. He had worked hard, and had been enterprising and determined. But there had been no impact.

He wasn't religious, and he had no moral compunctions. Yet, he had prayed. But nothing had changed. During the course of his miserable life, he had been told that positive thoughts led to positive developments. He was finally giving up on all spiel. His decision had become irrevocable.

However, he did not feel like carrying out his plan in the hustle bustle of the city. He needed peace and quiet and tranquility to give up his life. He believed in maintaining the dignity of dying. So, he became innovative and creative, even intrepid. He was going to murder himself in the most ingenious manner! He began his research with genuine enthusiasm. It was as if he was on to a fabulous, new, million dollar idea.

He scoured the Internet and studied the forests of central India for a whole month. He planned his route with amazing caution. He held discreet interviews with acquaintances from the forest department to get to know the terrain better. He slaved and slogged to get this going. He wanted glory.

When his trek began, he knew that he was doing remarkably well. He was on time, and on track. Slowly, he began leaving the noise and din of civilized life behind him. The marvelous sounds of the forest became clearer. The trees knew what he was up to; the birds could sense it, too. He did not see many people in the area. Those he did encounter were offered a palatable story. He was on a research mission.

In time, he found himself completely alone; there wasn't a soul for miles. He was happy. He took out his hip flask and took a swig. What a beautiful day it was! Pristine, tranquil and full of potential. Perhaps, he had made a mistake. Perhaps, he ought to drop the plan, and go back.

Just as these thoughts prevailed, he heard a male voice call out to him. You can imagine his consternation. He had just found the perfect spot. He was enjoying a drink. And here…!The voice belonged to a young, shaggy, city boy with a ponytail. He must've been twenty-three or twenty-four. He was in a pair of azure blue jeans with tear marks at the knees. He wore a t-shirt that carried the slogan, "Alea iacta est" (The dice is cast), attributed to Julius Caesar.

What was this kid doing here? Was he going to spoil Ullas's plans? Was he alone? Or, with friends? Uneasy and rattled, Ullas tried to question him. But the boy seemed so elated to see the older man that he did not pay any attention to the query. Instead, he came rushing forward with zeal. "I'm so glad to see you. I've been waiting here, in these parts for over a week now. And I do hope that you'll be able to help me," he said, panting and breathless.

The poor soul was lost in the forest, reckoned Ullas. He looked sun burnt and under-nourished. Pat began the interrogation—"What happened to you? Who are you? Are you stranded? Are there others with you? Is anyone hurt? Is there no one around to help you?"

The boy laughed. Ullas was both intrigued and annoyed. This was no time for frivolity. His thick eyebrows furrowed. The boy noticed the frown, and said, to Ullas's complete astonishment, "I'm not lost, Mister. I intended to be here."

He had a crooked, lop-sided smile. Ullas was curious. Why would a young city-bred want to be in the forest, all alone, and looking very harassed and shabby? "I don't understand. You say that you are here of your own accord. In that case, why have you sought me out? I have my own plans and would very much like to be left alone, young man," he said, admonishing the lad. "You are delaying me. I don't have all the time in the world, I say!" he added.

The youth looked at Ullas with a plea in his eyes. He seemed determined to bother his senior. Perhaps his plan was equally challenging. "I have a huge favour to ask of you, Sir," he said, mysteriously. "My name is Agraj. I'm a student, and I'm trying to commit suicide," he announced.

The wind went out of Ullas's sails. This pesky thing was ruining the novelty of his big task for the day. It wasn't going to be an 'exclusive' any more. "I'm afraid I don't understand," he managed to say, without showing too much surprise.

"You see, Sir, I came all the way from the city to be able to peacefully give up my life," said the boy. "Pardon my manners. I haven't even asked you for your name. How may I address you?" he asked, politely. Ullas immediately felt a surge of empathy for the boy but he had other things on his mind. He was not going to be swayed and lose track of his own assignment.

"So, where is the problem?' he retorted brusquely. He felt like another drink. "Just do your thing. No one will stop you. I won't bother you. In fact, I wish you the very best," he said, and tried to turn away. But the boy did not flinch. Instead he said, "It is most kind of you to give me your wishes, Sir. But there is a hitch. A crucial element of the plan has to fall in place, and I'm wondering whether you could help me with it."

This was getting more convoluted by the minute. Ullas was suddenly wise to the fact that his own plan might have to be shelved. He had enough food. It would last him for another forty-eight hours. So, he decided to help the boy fulfill his wish. He took out his flask, and took a healthy gulp. Then, he said, "Tell me how I can be of service to you, and I'll try to do my best." He meant that. It seemed noble to be able to help someone, particularly during those last, fainting hours of his own rotten life.

He had nothing else to look forward to. He was a failed actor, who had tried hard to get his act together, but in vain. He had had some luck, appearing in sundry local ads and doing the odd role in small budget movies but his utopian dream of making it big as a metropolitan superstar had evaded him. He had been told that he had neither the depth nor the substance and definitely not the looks to make it 'big'!

Ullas had finally taken on the role of an unseemly Petrarchan lover, who having rendered sonnet after limpid sonnet to his beloved, was now being promised…sweet redemption…death itself.

Agraj spoke, extricating the older man from the comfort of his blissful misery. "Please come with me to my spot," he urged. "I have made elaborate plans there. And, I'll need you so that I can succeed," he stressed. So, Ullas, a bit reluctantly, gathered his belongings, and followed the boy into the thicket.

After having walked for about forty minutes, he came upon a makeshift home that Agraj had built for himself. There was a table and a chair. Books were stacked neatly on one side of the table. There were papers and pens strewn about carelessly in the centre. A stainless steel coffee mug with a black handle was kept on the right hand corner of the desk. There was a small fire, a stove, some pots and pans. It looked divine.

The boy even had a three-piece drum set on display, the shebang…a bass drum, a hanging tom, a snare drum, hi-hats and a suspended cymbal. It was preposterous; absolutely incredible!

How on earth had this young boy lugged all that up into the hills, Ullas wondered! But he refrained from making further enquiries, in spite of the novelty and the freshness of his situation. He just wanted to do what he could, and skedaddle from there.

"Would you please take a seat? I have something very important to share with you," said the boy, sitting down on a boulder, and offering Ullas the chair. "I still don't know your name. Would you like to tell me," he began, gently. But Ullas was losing patience. "It doesn't matter. Just tell me what you want. I'll do it for you, and then, I'll be gone. I have things to do, too, and we can't spend the whole day pursuing your grandiose plans," he retorted sharply.

"In that case, I shall call you The Grim Reaper, and be done with that for the moment," said Agraj dramatically. Ullas was having a tough time being polite. This young boy had just told him that he was about to commit suicide. From his current state of mind, it seemed as if there had been a change in plan. "So, are you or are you not planning to commit suicide?" he prodded. He was getting edgy. "Just tell me your plan, and be done with it so that I can leave," he blurted.

"Just a minute, Sir," insisted Agraj. "Just a few minutes, and you'll be free of me," he said gently. He was mocking his senior. "You are already aware that I intend to commit suicide today. However, what I did not share with you earlier is that I want it to look like murder," he pointed out, dispassionately. Murder! What a marvelous idea, thought Ullas. Why hadn't he come up with that! Darn! These young guys were smart! "But why murder?" he asked. "What's wrong with suicide?"

Agraj looked at Ullas matter-of-factly. "Don't you get it, Mister? If I hang myself, it'll be boring. There's nothing new about hanging oneself. I don't know whether I can cut my throat swiftly enough to be able to die. I'm not that strong. If I shoot myself, will I die quickly or will I have to watch myself bleed to death? There's nothing very original about shooting oneself, either. I want a very novel death," he explained.

Ullas's head spun. He went pale. "Here, please have some tea, Mr Reaper, Sir. It'll refresh you," said the youngster. The concern was genuine but the name-calling irked him. "My name is Ullas Rai," he said, introducing himself, for the very first time. He suddenly felt connected to this young, enterprising lad, who had been meticulously planning his grand finale. He had reposed faith in this old stranger. Ullas couldn't let him down.

"Hmm. Let me see. You want your suicide to look like a murder! Is that it?" he confirmed. "Absolutely, Mr Rai. A simple murder to alleviate the taint associated with suicide. Those who are murdered get to keep their dignity. Those who commit suicide are seen as pathetic. Don't you agree?" he asked. Agraj did have a point. It would definitely be more interesting for those who knew him to receive a 'murder' story instead of a shameful 'suicidal' one.

The two men put their heads together and began working towards a foolproof plan to make this work. They had a little ammunition. Agraj had his uncle's rifle, a rope, a knife and some rat poison. All Ullas had was an old knife with a gold rimmed handle with a monogram of the sun on it. It was very handy, and its blade was sharp. Ullas wondered about the youngster's weapon, but said nothing.

"How about something to eat, first? I'm really famished, and can't think very clearly," he confessed. "In a minute, Mr Rai," said the lad, springing into action. He took out his pan, and some eggs, and onions and potatoes. They were going to have Spanish omelets in the wild. The day was turning into a picnic. "But I must not lose sight of my target," Ullas reminded himself. "I shall eat, and then help this poor chap die," he muttered to himself.

Scratching his head, Ullas tried to come up with the perfect murder cover for this suicide. He had become a little greedy, too. He now wanted this sort of thing for himself. "You know what, Agraj, I did not tell you this earlier but I, too, am on a similar mission," he revealed. The boy's eyes widened with astonishment. "Wow! Mr Rai, Isn't that great?" he said. "Imagine meeting someone like-minded in a place like this one," he added. Imagine indeed!

Ullas was curious though about why such a young boy was contemplating such a drastic step. "Tell me, why do you wish to die? You are so young," he asked. Agraj sighed. "There's no money at home. The family's in debt. My parents died recently in a house collapse. I have no support system and no future," he said, quite dismissively. He seemed to have made peace with his situation. Ullas felt sorry for the poor thing. He wanted to know more. "Give me the details," he encouraged.

"My father was a mason. His father, too, was one. It has been the family's profession for several generations," said Agraj. "But real power in the household rests with my father's elder brother, who handles all the finances and decides upon all work projects," he added. "My father borrowed a lot of money from my uncle to educate me. He also received a retainer from the man. Beyond that, he did not have an active role in my future," the boy explained.

"Ah! I see," responded Ullas. "Can't your uncle help you?" he enquired. Agraj looked crestfallen. "I doubt it," he said. "My uncle will support my future plans only if I give up my aspirations to study further and help him in the family business. All my cousins have been roped in, too. I'm the only black sheep in the family. So, you see how moribund all this is?" he asked. Ullas nodded. It was a cul de sac. But still, he felt that there was a way out. Someone ought to salvage the situation. Perhaps Agraj could get a scholarship or find a sponsor. Something. This boy must not be allowed to die, and for no fault of his.

Perhaps, he could help Agraj live, thought Ullas, for a moment. Or maybe, he ought not to try and ruin someone else's life, as well. He hadn't been very successful with his own. "Hope you don't mind. But I must catch my forty winks. When I wake up, we'll do something about your plan," he assured the boy, and lay down to rest. Agraj shut his eyes as well, and soon, two people, who had very important things to do that day, dozed off.

It was dark when Ullas awoke. He looked at his watch. They had been sleeping for three hours. "Wake up, boy," said Ullas. He looked at the innocence on Agraj's face. What a tragedy it would be to slit that throat! He couldn't do it.

He was going to have to change his plan. He was not going to die. And, he wouldn't let this young boy kill himself, either. He let him sleep. And decided to put everything off until the next morning.

The boy was livid. "How dare you suggest something this atrocious?" he shouted when Ullas told him about the new plan. "And, why didn't you wake me up last night?" he asked. "We've wasted an entire day now," he complained. "Mr Rai, give me your knife," he ordered. "No, Agraj. Please think again. Let us join forces and live under one roof. You could be my support system and I could be your guide, if you so wish," suggested Ullas. "You must not give up so soon. You have your whole life in front of you. I'm sure we could come up with some plan to help you realize your dreams," he said weakly.

"Bah!" replied Agraj. He was in no mood to change tack. His mind was set. He lunged at Ullas's rucksack and began throwing everything out of it; his notes, his diaries, some old letters; his wallet; pathetic cuttings from rickety newspapers—his whole life. The boy was looking for the knife, and he found it. He then brought out his own knife, and went up to a boulder. He began sharpening both knives with intensity. The look on his face made Ullas nervous. 'This crazy kid is actually going to kill himself and me,' he thought. Agraj then took out the rifle and began loading it.

Wasn't there anything he could do to change the boy's mind? He decided to try one more time to convince Agraj. He wanted to save him. "Look Agraj, I've changed my plan. Let us not give in! Let us survive! Let us take on fate, and let us win! Dying like thieves is ignominious," he began saying. But it was just too late by then. Agraj had positioned his rifle and was pointing it at Ullas.

The older man lunged for it. Agraj reacted. The bullet went past Ullas, ricocheted off a boulder and hit the pan and then the cymbal. All the metal fell down in a heap. There was much clanging and pealing. Such a racket! It echoed through the region. Both men fell on the ground, stunned and bruised but laughing. It was difficult to live. But it was even more tedious trying to die!

****

Network Junkie

Yudhvir Jhalani found himself unemployed, one day, after twenty years of continued slavery. It was a peculiar feeling, quite unfamiliar. But he came to enjoy the leisure and the absence of deadlines and pressures. The liberty to indulge and to be at odds with strict daily routines gave him untrammelled joy. As a media man, he had kept long hours and operated rather suspiciously. This, however, was different.

Untied from the yoke, he was now able to stay up watching a movie or listening to music until sunrise. Or, be found sleeping until sunset. For the first few weeks, he found himself enjoying this freedom so much that he took no offence when acquaintances called to check upon his "well-being". He assured them that he was fine and told them that he was going to take it easy for a while. His lament was that the world doesn't let you be unless you fit into one of its many silos. "I'm going to chart my own course from here," he would say.

Yuvi had been an odd-ball for a long time. It was only now that he was making it public. One couldn't take his words at face value. He was an unapologetic, compulsive liar, who concocted sketchy yarns, and concealed information. It seemed as if he was always in some inexplicable, unfathomable, mysterious trouble. His gaze was flighty and his movements, restive. It was as if he were a spy, out and about, incognito.

To be able to see him at close quarters, you'll have to 'get' what I'm about to tell you here. I once visited him at his workplace. We took a long flight of stairs up to his first floor cabin. En route, he told me, winking, that his latest trip abroad was a "classified" assignment to Kabul. He couldn't give me the details, of course. Just then, he bumped into a colleague of his and began talking very secretively. He threw nervous glances at me and his eyebrows were furrowed.

Assuming that he wanted privacy, I moved away. When he joined me a few minutes later, he began trashing the guy. "That cheapskate! Who the hell does he think he is!" I surmised that the man in question was not an ally. "Oh no.

He's a very dear friend but he won't lose any opportunity to undercut me," explained Yuvi. Journalists take cushy assignments very seriously. They work hard to keep the concerned parties in good humour so that when the time comes, they get that all-paid for trip abroad, somewhere. "I'm quite chummy with our boss. So, the chances of this chap upsetting my plan are slim," he noted. I nodded faintly.

Yuvi opened the glass door that led to his cabin, which was at the end of a long corridor, full of newspersons. Ducking his head at a senior obsequiously, he gave him a thumbs up, and said, "Great show, boss. That was a brilliant assessment. Even the exit polls got it wrong. Your promotion is now assured." The man beamed. The ego needs constant boosting. A few seconds later, however, I heard Yuvi whisper into my ear, "Good job or not, this one is going to get the sack very soon."

I had no one idea why he functioned like that. It might have been the nature of his job. Who knew! But the office receptionist, whom he greeted every day in Sindhi, was inordinately fond of him. She brought him tea and samosas every evening, and shared sweets from her lunch box every now and then. The reporters on his team liked him, too. He was polite and humble, and had "friends and contacts" everywhere. Was that an act? Or, was it natural?

I do not know. "It's all in the networking, my friend. No compunctions. No question of ethics. Just keeping adding the numbers. That'll come in handy someday," he would tell me repeatedly.

Yuvi's family was originally from Sindh in Pakistan but it had moved to Pune in Maharashtra, and located itself in Salisbury Park. His father was an artist and his mother, a jewellery maker. His twin sisters also worked in the media—one for radio and the other for television. But he was rather secretive about his people. For many years, he had given everyone the impression that his father worked for the Prime Minister's Office. You can imagine how misleading his gestures and moves must have been for this to have happened.

As for his love life, the more said… the better. Every new woman he fell for became the 'great new love of his life'. Each episode lasted for about six months. He would obsess over her; make furtive calls; bunk office to meet her; the works! Each one of these women was introduced to us with a knowing wink; which indicated—She is the one! And, when he moved on… the explanation was predictable—She wasn't the one!

I came to know this fickle, fretful, illegible lunatic when we were both cub reporters, years ago. We were covering one of those long-drawn, frigid political party briefings where uproarious, canny narcissists would regularly gather to tell media persons that they had finally taken the decision to 'not take a decision' on the "almost-decision"! This amorphous non-information was then read out so slowly that even the most incompetent scribe could jot it down. It would then be taken back to the office and conveyed to the seniors, and carried in the papers, the day after.

I can't quite remember how we were introduced but I do remember getting the sense that Yuvi was extremely well-connected and quite beloved. He was affable when he was sane, and very social. He was tall—almost six feet three inches; he stooped a bit; was slightly built, and had a thick black crop on his head. His eyebrows were quite pronounced. His nose was a caricaturist's delight, and his jaw protruded. The first time I saw him he was taking notes on small scraps of paper and stuffing them into the pockets of his trouser, and he kept looking left and right shiftily. He was on to an "exclusive"—a scoop in the journalism business—something to die for!

When I first met him, he and I worked for rival newsmagazines until I shifted loyalties. He had just had a great run with a breaking news kind of story and was being feted and envied by his peers. He took me under his wing and tried to make me feel comfortable in that large, cold, awe-inspiring place. That was when we connected. We also came up with some wonderful 'special' reports together. He easily charmed his way into my mother's heart and was soon a friend of the family, often turning up unannounced for festival lunches and dinners.

After some years in the print medium, he moved to the electronic medium and I moved away from journalism. So, it was quite heartening to bump into him on Facebook, the other day. We quickly 'be-friended' each other, and caught up for drinks one evening. Yuvi smoked like a chimney and drank until he passed out and had to be escorted home. He hadn't married. Thank Heavens! There was no one to badger and berate him for returning at dawn at least five times a week.

He was quite surprised that I had taken to writing fiction but was expressly supportive. "I think it's good. You're trying something new. Perhaps you'll create something useful," he deigned. Soon, he began reading my pieces. He may or may not have liked them but he made significant suggestions. He was a keen judge of the written word, and could make a fair assessment. He was brutally candid, too, and that helped.

But, after a while, he became awfully intrusive. He was always online, and he would post these really long preachy comments on anything anyone wrote. And the double games he played also continued. He had about 5,000 "friends" on Facebook and commented on nearly every post he laid eyes on. One had to only gently make an entry, and there he would be, tailing you.

He'd carry essays and write-ups (political propaganda) that he supported, and expected his "contacts" to endorse them. If they didn't, there'd be a terse note via a private message, commanding them to do so. These "orders" got more pressing during the run-up to the general elections in 2014 when the country began getting polarized on ideological grounds.

Yuvi was a left liberal; a staunch one at that. Brought up in the Nehruvian mould, he had a quaint view of secularism and on the State's social responsibility. A wave of nationalism sweeping the country during that year made him jittery, and he thwarted "fundamentalism" of any kind. The Hindutva-touting saffron brigade—these right-wingers screaming national pride and calling for the dismantling of "foisted western" values were anathema to him.

I, like many of my ilk, was a moderate liberal, standing just a little left of Centre, comfortable with neither the soft peddling of subsidies nor with the complete domination of cold market forces; not ill at ease with the shrill voice of patriotism but reluctant to be "non-secular" in the old context; not content with the State's intervention in everything and calling for its complete separation from religion; fascinated with capitalism and not in favour of a dependency culture but curious about how governments could achieve social equality.

Agreed that this is neither here nor there, being a hotchpotch of opinions that sometimes do not resonate with one another. But I couldn't get too jingoistic about either position. There were policies on both sides that I admired. Equally, there were announcements by practitioners of each doctrine that I was loathe to accept. In any case, I was far more apt to play the part of the observer, who was willing to endorse a humanitarian Right or a more practical Left.

It was under these tenuous circumstances that Yuvi and I had re-connected. I noticed that he was patronizing one particular politician a lot, and was prone to carrying his "thoughts" and "speeches" verbatim. This man spewed vitriol on the opposition and claimed that in spite of all the noise in the country, the status quo of the incumbent government wasn't being challenged.

I opposed that, and wrote counters, taking him head on. This was not just for entertainment but for the purpose of debate and in the name of veracity. Impressionable youth in large numbers was lapping up the content put out on the Net. Therefore, both sides needed to be presented. In any case, any journalist worth his salt will have an opinion and will make that available to anyone willing to entertain it. And even though I had moved away from journalism, the bug remained. I did see what the experts were saying—that our country was far more divided on caste lines rather than on ideological terms.

This pow-wow between opinions continued, with Yuvi standing by the politician mentioned above, and I, refusing to change my stance. After a long and noisy campaign, in which many friendships went through testing times and several latent differences revealed themselves, the right wing surged ahead, victorious. Yuvi was heart-broken. I was equidistant from both ideologies but not entirely nonchalant about the outcome. Yuvi couldn't understand that position.

He was also fully determined to stand-by his politician friend. He sent him condolence messages on public platforms and didn't forget to remind him that this wasn't the end of the world. He himself wrote voluble treatises on why the election results did not indicate the emergence of a new political atmosphere in the country. His blogs were equally vociferous about the lack of a dent on leftist persuasions.

This continued for a few weeks in a highly charged environment. I decided not to engage anymore. Instead, I planned to watch how the new set-up was to unfold. It had been a volatile phase, which had witnessed terribly emotional outbursts from all sides. Some detachment was in order, and I was going to purge myself of all the hubbub and babel. I also noticed that Yuvi's politico buddy was beginning to tire out, and even ignored Yuvi's incessant "support". Yuvi, on the other hand, kept at it, challenging the new government's so-called popularity, based on relatively low vote share figures, despite the victory.

The overall ambience in the country was one of celebration. The new government was sworn-in with much grandeur and flourish, and the wheels of an alternative method of governance were set in motion. Politics-mongers across the nation continued to discuss and debate the results at dinners and social functions. Meanwhile, the staunch, (allegedly) Left-leaning, ambitious politico quietly shifted loyalties and conveyed his openness to join the opposition's ranks.

Yuvi's buddy did the impossible, and was accepted by his opponents. Having gone over to the other side, he was now disinclined to Yuvi's friendship. Meanwhile, Yuvi's employers abruptly gave him the boot, and asked him to vacate his chair within twenty-four hours. Several years of arrogance and innocence came crashing down in that one instance. Not being one to give up so easily, Yuvi threatened legal action against the management, and is still fighting that battle. But on that pitiful day, he had to collect the shattered fragments of his dignity and walk out of that building, all alone.

Some months passed by before I got a message from him. "Do you want to catch up?" he asked. "I am leaving for Kochi. A Malayalam TV channel has offered me a job. It isn't much and the pay is pathetic. But I'm taking it anyway. At least it is better than having nothing to do. Besides, who knows when I'll find a decent job in Delhi again," he said. I sent him a congratulatory message. I couldn't meet him because I was travelling. But I told him that I was glad that he was back in the saddle.

"Visit me when you are in the city," he extended a courteous invitation. "I hear that the food is worth trying out," he added on a lighter note. He was never much of a foodie and normally ate little.

"Thanks, I will," I said, adding, "But…in the interim, won't we be in touch… on the social media etc.?" His response was cryptic. "I've had enough of that. I don't think I'm going to be there; not for a long, long time."

****

The Pirates of Aden

Andor Grof is a 28-year-old, light-skinned, curly-haired Hungarian shippy, nick-named 'Ace'. He has encountered some turbulent times during the last six years on his trips across the seas. But he loves being a mariner. Being on a large tanker surrounded by water and with no land in sight for days on end can be nerve-wracking but that is the life he has chosen, and he's up for it. He confessed, however, that one incident left him reasonably shaken. Seated at a bar in Tenerife in the Canary Islands, he begins to tell me the story.

Here it is…in his own words.

It was sometime in mid-2007. This was my twelfth trip on the seas. I was east-bound on the Gulf of Aden (GOA) and coming out from the Suez Canal. You're aware of the Gulf?

My response may not have convinced him. So, he went on to give the details.

It is located in the Arabian Sea between Yemen, in the southern coast of the Arabian Peninsula and Somalia, in the Horn of Africa, and it connects with the Red Sea in the north-west through the Bab-el-Mandeb Strait, which is only about 20 miles wide; a perilously narrow alley. Being on the GOA is no mean task.

I nodded. He had just ordered himself some apricot rakia.

As the waterway is a part of the important Suez Canal shipping route between the Mediterranean Sea and the Arabian Sea in the Indian Ocean, more than 20,000 ships cross the gulf annually. It 'has' to be traversed because it is a shorter route. But being on the stretch is a high-alert job. As mariners, we are given special orientation sessions on how to tackle events here. Every sailor must also be prepared for the worst, and perform at his best, when the need arises… and that happens often.

That is because 'Pirate Alley' is known for its notorious inhabitants, who have become more and more aggressive over the years. The pirates, who hang around this region, are highly motivated, well-trained and armed with enough ammunition to cause a scare. Although it is not to their advantage to damage the vessel they intend to capture, they carry RPG (rocket-propelled grenade) guns, too. Vessels are often captured here and on the east coast of Somalia and taken to anchorages, off Eyl and Hobyo, to be ransomed. And, most such activity happens around dawn or dusk.

As for my vessel, it was a Very Large Crude Carrier—a VLCC—all of 370 metres from bow to stern and 58 metres wide. If you were to hold her vertically from top to toe, she would comfortably upstage the Eiffel Tower. She looked majestic, even from a distance. `The Blue Whale' was ginormous and beautiful, and she had been painted a rich blue and grey.

He had become nostalgic. I took a sip of my Greyhound, lit a cigar, and waited for him to go on.

Once on the ship, I met the rest of the crew members. We were twenty-seven in all. There were six deck officers including the captain, six engineers including the chief engineer, eight deck hands, four engine room helpers and three people in charge of catering. The group was a smorgasbord of Ukrainians, Bulgarians, Serbs, Croatians, and some Indian and Philippine nationals. An interesting bunch.

We were carrying the mother of all cargoes—Oil. That meant a large amount of loading and unloading, and enough paper work for me. The administrative work is routine and mundane but it has to be done. I was in charge of communications and the management of funds on board. Stores were under my supervision and so was allocation. I spent my free time on the bridge and learnt about radars. They fascinated me.

I would often join my Chief Officer at seven every morning for a cup of coffee. Then, I'd get ready and begin work at eight. We had struck up a rapport and our connection was buoyant and crackling. Chief Mate Faust Horvat was a decent looking, well-sculpted, 32-year-old Croatian; a quick-witted man of many talents. He was a foodie, a musician and a master craftsman. One could find him during off-hours, carving catapults out of wood and painstakingly making Turkish guns from iron pipes. He also played the flute.

On natty evenings, he filled up the living room with music. But at work, he was fastidious; religiously handing down responsibilities to the ratings every day. He also kept the deck hands productively occupied. Horvat was a reliable man in any situation, or so I had heard. I do believe that our mutual fascination for music and food drew us close. He named me Ace.

Horvat would be on watch from 4 to 8 every morning and each evening, and looked forward to some conversation time with me. (Watch hours are divided into six slots of four hours each and the three officers did two slots each). For an hour after his watch, the Chief Officer would be in the galley, poring over what was cooking, and making suggestions. The food was humble fare but Horvat would often work his magic into a meal.

He rarely slept for more than four hours at a stretch. He was always up and about; fresh and full of energy. And, he hadn't had an 'incident' in quite some time. But on that morning, just as he took charge of the watch, he was informed by the navigator about a probable intruder in the vicinity. He picked up the intercom and called me. "Ace! Do you think you could join me earlier today?'

We were about 250 nautical miles from land. The sea was calm. We were cruising. I looked at the alarm-clock on my bedside table. It was 4.10 am. He must have just come on watch. Was there a crisis? Why would he call me? "Come to the bridge! You've got to see this," he insisted. Knowing Horvat, I knew it was important.

He took a bite of the papas arrugadas and mojo rojo (wrinkled potatoes and red salsa) before telling me—"I rushed to the Wheel House. The wheel that steers the ship rests here. It is the highest point on the ship—a terrace." I bobbed my head. He went on....

"What's up, Chief?" I asked. "Come on over," Horvat beckoned. His voice had urgency. "Weren't you curious about mother vessels? This is what a mother vessel looks like," he said, pointing to a blip on the radar. There was an 'icon' there, indicating that we had 'company'; unwanted company.

This was going to be an assault and attack story. I am ashamed to say that I was excited. I could feel my blood pressure rising. My ears felt warm. He explained....

'Mother vessel' is the term used to denote ships used by pirates at sea. These are yachts, often fishing boats. That makes their identification quite difficult. One has to watch out for specific activity taking place from the yacht to smaller, high speed craft called 'skiffs'. These are rafts, usually two or three in number. Pirates are deployed from the mother vessel on to these skiffs when the plan to attack is launched.

I looked at the icon on the radar once more, trying to grasp the enormity of what would soon become a 'situation'. Meanwhile, Horvat addressed the Able Seaman (AB) and said, "Check carefully." The AB, who was at the steering wheel, also looked surprised. He peered through a pair of high-powered binoculars and saw three skiffs bob about in the water. These rafts do not have much fuel in them but they are fast, going up to speeds of 25 knots per hour. "I can see people getting off the yacht on to the skiffs," he announced.

To check the nature of the pirates, Horvat then asked the AB to look at the shape of the boat. "You see, both

Yemeni fishermen and Somalian pirates can be found in small boats here but the main difference between the boats is the shape of the bow," he explained. "The Yemeni boats have a sharp, uplifted bow with a pronounced rake while the Somalian pirate boats usually have a blunt bow like that of a ship's lifeboat. And, both boats are powered by outboard motors. Moreover, Yemeni boats can travel at speeds of up to 25 knots while Somalian boats can touch about 30 knots," he elaborated.

I was on to a Moscow Mule by now...and was feverishly picking on some churros de pescado. I couldn't wait for the rest of this tale. Ace continued...

Once it had been better established that we needed help, Horvat asked me to call Second Officer Dejan Babic, who was both the ship's navigator and its medical officer. He was also in charge of maintaining the distress signaling equipment such as the Global Maritime Distress Safety System (GMDSS). The Serb's watch had been over at 4 am but he came back to post. No one could take it easy while this operation was launched. He went back on the radar.

The radar could see everything in a vicinity of up to 12-15 nautical miles around it, and it had determined that the pirate craft were coming towards us at a speed of 28 knots per hour. We could see many yellow dots go up on the green screen. On any other day, we would have known that these were harmless fishing boats, sail boats or yachts. But today, we knew what they meant. In the engine room, Chief Engineer RK Ugathy had already made it clear to his staff that we could need engines at full power. "Keep the second generator running on stand-by mode," he had ordered.

Convinced that this was an emergency, Horvat asked me to inform the Master. Olek Tereshchenko, a 59-year-old Ukranian, with twenty-seven years experience as captain and thirty-five years on the seas, had seen it all. He was a bulky man with a bushy beard and crooked teeth. The minute he was shown the radar and the vessel in the distance, the captain knew what it was. The next few hours were going to be eventful.

"Call the engine room," the captain ordered, and asked if Chief Engineer Ugathy had been informed. When the connection was made, he announced, "The con is with me." The captain was in charge from that moment. "Is the second generator ready?" he asked. The Blue Whale could go up to a speed of 18 knots per hour, when loaded, and to about 22 knots, when not loaded. (Container ships can go even faster, at about 30-32 knots.) And, we were still carrying some load.

I quite enjoyed dawn. But not today.

Ace took a swig of his Cuba Libre. We were having a

cocktail fiesta, and mixing up our drinks.

The pirate vessel had begun approaching us. It was time to up the ante. News that something was amiss had spread. The captain took some decisions. He said that we were to move on course. Everyone was to be at work. "Take wheel on hand," he told the AB. Auto mode was to be removed, and operation handled manually.

The sailor in charge of looking out for intrusion, attack or collision on the port side could see the skiffs moving determinedly towards us. There were two such sailors (lookouts) on the ship, one each on the left and the right side. Captain Chenko asked the lookout on the starboard side to also come to the left. And, we increased our speed from 13 knots to 15 knots. It would, however, take about 15 minutes for the increased RPM to come into effect on such a large machine. "Call UKMTO and inform them that we suspect an attack on our vessel," the captain told me.

"The United Kingdom Maritime Trade Office (UKMTO), Dubai; the Joint Task Force of the Horn of Africa and the Maritime Liaison Office, Bahrain, have to be tapped as soon as a ship suspects an attack of this sort. A Mayday alert goes out on VHF Channel 16, which the pirates sometimes try to jam by playing music on it," he revealed. "I contacted the naval forces, who indicated that it would take about 20 minutes for them to get to our assistance by chopper. This meant we would have to defend the ship for that time period, aggressively," he stressed.

I couldn't imagine being in a situation like that. I drank some more, and waited for him to go on.

The Master sounded the alarm—seven short blasts followed by a long blast. Every sailor would know that this was an emergency and come to the muster station, on the main deck. The captain picked up the Public Address System and announced, "We suspect an attack." I saw some deck hands shift nervously in their red boiler suits. "There is no need to panic. Just follow the drill. Implement everything you have learnt. If you freeze now, you will not see your families for a long time. So, start defending the ship…now," he ordered.

His message had the desired effect; and even the weak-kneed gathered resolve. No one wanted to be captured. We had heard of such incidents. The modus operandi of the pirates was to identify their target in the GOA; wait for dawn, creep up on a large, loaded ship and seize one that could not defend itself, and then drive up a hard bargain. They often used rifles and hand grenades during the attack, and latched on to ladders or grappling lines to gain access to the deck.

Their effort was to get a ransom equivalent to the worth

of the ship, the crew and the cargo. Large ships are worth a lot of money; carrying up to 2 lakh metric tons of oil. Each tank of oil could be worth anything up to 30,000 dollars. My ship had 10 such tanks. The bargaining process could go on for two-three months. In the beginning, for about 10 days, there is no talk. And, then, the negotiations begin. It is a tiresome process, and quite harrowing, too. Our minds were made up. We were not going to surrender.

He fell silent, and began fiddling with the food on his plate. I realized that this was painful for him. I decided to excuse myself for a while and was about to get up when he spoke again…

We looked out for the pirates, and noticed that they were heading towards us from the front. "Let's go for a head-on collision," ordered the captain. They must have been at a distance of about six miles, which was quite close. When they realized that the ship was taking an aggressive stance, they decided to change their approach. "We are not slowing down," the captain asserted. "Maintain course. Maintain speed," he ordered. We continued to move ahead on a head-on collision course.

From the corner of my eye, I saw Horvat take a quick look at a locket that hung around his neck. It had pictures of his 3-year-old son and of his lovely wife, who was carrying their second child. I wondered what was going through his mind but he looked absolutely calm and determined, and just as aggressive as Captain Chenko, if not more. The ship moved straight ahead, without any intention of slowing down. The pirates, who are known to be agile and quick, were also aware of taking on such a huge vessel from the front. So, they retreated. But the seniors knew that this wasn't going to be the end of it.

"They'll be back," cautioned Babic. He had, in the past, been on a vessel which had been captured. He had spoken about the incident to me. He had told me that all the pirates wanted was the money. They had treated the crew with complete indifference as if they were cargo, not human beings. "They were not cruel or inhuman but they could've become violent at any given point in time. There was fear and uncertainty," he had reminisced.

The bar kept plying us with liquor...It was a booze fest... Caipirinha, Up Town Twists, Daiquiri... We were getting drunk ...but unwilling to stop the volley. So, what happened? Did the pirates return? Did they, I asked him. He looked at me, puzzled...and said...

Sure enough, the pirates returned! Keeping an eye on the approach of the skiffs was challenging. One mistake could have been our undoing. Meanwhile, Third Officer Antonin, who was in charge of all safety equipment including life-saving and fire fighting appliances, had dispatched distress messages to the concerned authorities via the Ship Security Alert System. The message mentioned the vessel's current position, course and speed, among other necessary details.

We were, by then, to go to the open (choppy) seas, which swell more. There is a 36 hour stretch near the Gulf of Aden, and then, it is on to the Indian Ocean. "Sound the alarms," ordered the Master. These horns are audible up to a distance of 12-14 miles and are used liberally during such incidents to send distress messages to ships in the vicinity, particularly warships. They also alert the Coast Guard. "Let's send the pirates a message," said the captain. "Let's tell them that we know that they're coming. Our manoeuvres should be aggressive," he stressed.

The pirates had decided to attack us from the rear, this time. But because of the 'funnel' at the rear end of the ship, the radar couldn't see them very well. They were tagging along in that area. A two mile patch just behind the ship falls into the Radar Blind Area.

I see, I said. The information coming to me was fascinating.

So, targets have to be spotted visually. And, the attackers are aware of this and they were trying to take advantage. But, for every move, there would be a counter move.

"Send a lookout with Antonin," said the Master. The infrared binoculars were put to work. And the Third Mate confirmed, "Quarters' end—from behind. We switched off the extra lights so that they could not see us. "There are six in each raft," Antonin said. We had to hold on for another 10 minutes. The Second Mate was still in contact on the VHF. I was talking to UKMTO and to my company. And it was nearly dawn when music began playing on Channel 16. The rogues had jammed the frequency.

I heard him pull his breath. He took out his pipe and began filling it. I waited quietly. He then took out his tamper, compressed the tobacco, and when he was visibly satisfied with the process, he lit it up. He drew on it leisurely…and pressed on….

"Go for the Wake," ordered the captain. The ship was to first turn 5 degrees left and then 5 degrees right. This would slow down its speed by 2 knots but it would create such powerful waves that it would not be easy for anyone to attack, he explained. *I shook my head.*

"They are not giving up yet. They have inched even closer to us, about 4 miles," said Horvat. Meanwhile, the hoses tied to the railing of the ship were prepared for use. These hoses, tied from mid ship to the rear, were to be fired with water, to create mist and moisture. At the rear end, there were sawdust bags, which were also about to be used.

"Wear your goggles and throw the sawdust with as much force as possible," Captain Chenko ordered. This could cause a lot of irritation in the eyes and even permanent damage.

Two deck hands cut the sawdust and began throwing it in the air. One raft slowed down but the others were speeding up. We fired up our hoses, ready to launch them on the attackers. Sometimes, just keeping these hoses ready makes all the difference. Speed is of essence.

"We have orders to be severe. We have to show that we are not afraid. We must also convey our readiness for a fight. There is no room for complacency now or for anything lackadaisical," reminded the captain. Just then, the pirates fired their first salvo with RPG guns. If we slipped even a little, they would get to dominate. We knew that. So, each and every man on the ship was determined to fight hard.

The grenade missed the bridge but landed in the waters close by, causing a huge splash. Had it hit us, someone would have been injured for sure. But pirates do not wish to cause physical damage to a vessel or to its crew; they see them as valuable assets, to be overpowered and used for ransom later.

The RPG must have been fired only as a scare tactic. They began gaining on us, zipping over the waves at 25 knots. Our speed was 13 knots. "Topple them over! If they get on this ship, we'll be taken prisoners," thundered Horvat. He was enraged. We began creating zigzag maneuvers to form waves. We also used catapults to lance metal bolts in the direction of our pursuers. We had no guns. This was our only ammunition.

My bare feet felt the black sand on the beach for the first time. It was a luminous day. The nudists were looking for coves. I saw them but my mind was trying to visualize what Ace must've endured. So, they gave up the chase? I prodded.

Pirates don't give up the chase. They do this all the time. Why would they give up now? asked Ace.

Their rafts moved deftly; speeding up and slowing down intermittently. They must've been weighing their options. Were they about to speed up, latch on to the ladders by the ship and climb aboard? Or, were they going to take a hit and retreat? The wake created by the ship had made it quite difficult for them to come close to it. The metal parts were still flying at them with great force, and enough sawdust was being thrown into the air. This ship was not ready to cave in.

We hung by the skin of our teeth, and then, we heard the naval choppers arrive. There was hope now. One of them came to the ship. "Go and get them," commanded the Master. Horvat and I went to the helipad to receive them. "I think we'll be fine now," he assured me. I smiled at him.

Three gunmen trooped on board, moving with expertise through the ship. They positioned themselves on the stern (the rear end) and began firing. And the other chopper, which hovered above us, began taking down the rafts, which had slowed down. One raft went left, scurrying for cover and another went right. And the third took a hit. The entire corridor was now covered. We had ample help. They retreated for good.

I let out a huge sigh of relief. My croquetas caseras and chopitos had been altogether neglected. And, I needed another drink.

"I had never encountered this sort of a battle before and kept getting the gnawing feeling that they would come back but that did not happen. Instead, we heard that another ship had been attacked and captured by the same gang about 12-13 hours after that, in the same position, where the raft had sunk. Horvat was distraught," Ace recalled.

Captain Chenko consoled him. "We are all aware of the dangers of being on this patch. We are cautioned repeatedly and regularly, and we also have instructions on what to do. Some of us manage to do so, and yet others are not so fortunate. But let's be hopeful about their fate," he said, urging his Chief Officer to regain his balance. Later that morning, he broke some wine on the hull to celebrate. His aggressive stance and the support of the crew had saved the ship.

"You know, my grandfather, who was also a mariner, had once told me—No matter what happens in life, keep the courage! When I was a young boy, it did not make much sense. But over the last thirty years, through stormy weather and through catastrophe, I've come to truly understand and appreciate what he meant," he told the crew.

We were standing on the poop deck (the rear deck, just behind the bridge). I saw some playful dolphins go by. "These are bearers of good news, Ace. I do hope we'll get some," he said, and laughed. The next morning, I saw a white seagull fly by. That, too, was a good sighting. The 'adventure' was over, he reminisced.

Many days after that, I kept wondering about what might've happened had we been captured. Several hundred seafarers have been taken hostage by the Somalian pirates, who infest the seas, across which 90 per cent of all trade takes place. Would my employers have paid the ransom? Would the pirates have sacrificed me? Who knows! But here I am, yet again, getting ready to board another ship. We'll be hitting the GOA again. My heart is aflutter. I am preoccupied. But I guess we'll just cross the Gulf… when we come to it. Wish me luck!

So, I raised my glass to him, thanked him for having shared his story with me, and said, "Salud! Y Amor! Y tiempo para disfrutarlos! Chin! Chin!"

(To Health and to Love! And…to Time to enjoy them! Cheers!)

****

The Begum of Ballimaran

One had to admit it. She was beautiful...and...in a very provocative sort of way. Her allure wasn't stagnant and uneventful like standing water in a pond. She was an enchantress. She was always aware of what she was doing, who she was engaging, and what she wanted in return. A woman with that sort of endowment! Very powerful! With her kohl-smeared eyes and her inviting, flirtatious gaze, she attracted sufficient attention, and used her artistry well on the opposite sex.

True, she was heavy. *Vatsyayana's Kamasutra* classifies women into categories—small, medium and large. She was on the larger side. But she wasn't the least bit self-conscious about herself, and waltzed about with great ease. Her gait was rather languid and unhurried. She went about her work in the manner of someone very self-assured and insouciant. Men ended up loving her to distraction; some of them becoming her humble slaves. The women she encountered could have been sorely contemptuous of her. Or so, I suspect. There was some evidence of the fact that wives lost their husbands to her charm and that these meetings (where all three were present) ended in bitter acrimony.

She was a renowned *khayal* singer from a famous *gharana* in North India and her *mehfils* went 'chock-a-block' full. She had a long retinue of admirers who bent over one another to fulfil her every wish and command. As is the case with the creative sorts, she was deliciously unpredictable and very, very appealing. She was in her late thirties. She had never married, declaring time and again that marriage was but a contract between two men—the father of the bride and the prospective groom…both of whom were simply trading "property".

She lived in one of the few remaining heritage mansions in *Ballimaran* in old Delhi surrounded by the sights and sounds and fragrances of history and nostalgia, and served by her *khansamas* (gourmet chefs), *khadims* and *mulazims* (male servants). Most had lived with her for over a decade and wouldn't leave, neither for praise nor for pelf. So smitten were they by her that even though she chastised them regularly, none blinked an eye. The admonitions were mostly about the spice in her food or the choice of saree laid out to wear. *Begum Sahiba* liked her food pungent and her sarees heavily embroidered and in bright colours.

Her mornings began with the ritualistic *riyaaz* at the break of dawn, followed by a hearty breakfast with her hangers-on, who began trooping into the *haveli* by 8 am. Undeterred and unfazed by what it would do to her throat or to her voice, the Begum would gorge on jalebis and imartis from a local *halvai* (sweets maker) and on greasy poori and halva. The hookah would come out and so would some poetry.

Enthusiastic, young wannabe bards thronged this durbar so as to be able to have her react to their work, and subsequently seek her patronage. She gave it graciously. Each new, desperate scribe was heard and the best of the lot selected. These men were later showcased during an evening *mehfil* or during a *mushaira*. The Begum was invited to a host of these events. She was hugely popular and had a sizeable network of consumers.

She had a close group of women friends who spent at least one day of every week with her, piling up on a large *divan* in her living room. Boisterous, loud, vibrant women who laughed all afternoon, and smoked and drank a great deal. They were given to dancing and to teasing one another.

There was much loose talk and gossip, several heated discussions on what was happening to the old city and some interactions on politics. There was enough food on the table, and post-lunch massages, followed by a skinny dip in the in-house Turkish *hamaam* bath. The windows of the large, airy room would remain open. The world outside could ogle, as it did. But the women didn't care.

Begum Sahiba, in particular, called Queen Bee by her friends, repeatedly said that women ought to be able to do just about anything they wanted to, and was melancholy that the world did not function that way. She had herself rebelled against her parents when they had tried to force her to marry, and wasn't enamored of her peers who wanted to do nothing but that. She often spoke of the need for women to be mentally independent, above all, and lost no opportunity to make her views public.

During her contemplative "moods", she wrote heart-wrenching poems, which she wouldn't publish for some reason. She was comfortable sharing them with these friends. Her disillusionment with the male gender pained her and caused her heartburn. She had loved freely through her teens and twenties, and devoted herself to her long retinue of lovers only to be betrayed by them. "The innocence of love died early for me," she had told one of her fans. "The fact that all love is transient hit me at a young age," she had added.

Urdu poetry is, traditionally, rife with descriptions of woe and pathos and longing. The lover is inflamed with passion and writes reams about his beloved, describing her beauty and her looks. She continues to be inaccessible, cruel even; and his love is rarely requited. From there begins his steady desolation until he is completely destroyed; doomed. And thus, is born a worthy poet. Only in this case, the roles had reversed. Begum Sahiba spared no man, and wrote rather candidly about his "wavering" interest in the fair sex.

Given this context, when I, a bedraggled *shayar* (poet) from Kanpur, came to *Purani Dilli* (old Delhi), looking for patronage, I was advised by my peers to pay my respects to her. There was so much mystery and exotica around the persona of this patron Begum that I just had to go and see her. Armed with all my poems, each one of them, and unable to find anything decent to wear, I entered the *haveli,* as I was. When my turn came, I read out a poem in that vein (the purposelessness of love) with all the feeling in my heart. She noticed me right away, and gave me her undivided attention.

The Begum was known to be generous even if she was eccentric. I was to experience quite a few things for the first time that day. She beckoned me to sit right next to her while the other readings went on, and then insisted that I stay back. One by one, as the visitors started exiting the place, I had a fair idea of what could transpire but that did not deter me. I wouldn't miss such an opportunity for anything in the world! She served me more wine. And we sat in her ante-chamber all afternoon, getting drunk, with only poetry and each other for company.

There was more to it. It was bound to happen, I guess. She came close to me as I recited my poems and touched my arm. It wasn't lascivious at all; just very genteel and affectionate. She must've liked what she had heard. Her eyes were moist; the *pallu* of her *saree* had fallen away and her ample bosoms spilled out of her blouse but she didn't seem to notice. She was spontaneously surrendering to her desire. She didn't need anyone's permission. I did the same.

Yes, I had a wife waiting for me back home. Yes, I was taking a risk. Yes, being with her was heavenly. No. I hadn't fallen in love with her. Neither did she believe in such "skirmishes". She did things impromptu and was content to cast all convention aside. I was thrilled to be in the arms of a woman who wasn't coy or unpretentious. It was refreshing. She knew what she wanted and took it without hesitation. These "morals" weren't shocking or objectionable. The woman who made love to me was an empowered, libertarian one, who had no qualms about the way she lived or behaved.

I knew right then that these "rules" of "correct"

behavior, which had been forced upon women through centuries of mental conditioning and emotional and physical imprisonment, ought to be knocked down and felled. An unleashed woman in all her glory was far more exciting than the deaf, mute, subservient sort. So, when I saw that the Begum had not let such precepts limit her identity and freedom, I was captivated.

The fact that she was sexually-liberated and fearless was her strength. I'm sure that is what drew so many men to her. Seduced by that independence, they groveled at her feet of their own accord. This wasn't a woman hiding behind a veil of false modesty and social norms and expectations. This one was living life to the hilt, and enjoying it, too. That couldn't be wrong! I could imagine being in the midst of my pathetic friends again, discussing this, and being booed off. Independent women didn't go too far without provoking slander, they would say.

It was no different with the Begum. Such a celebrated singer from such an exalted *gharana!* There had to be stories about her! She was bold and daring, and remarkably talented. There had to be some envy. The tabloids and magazines pursued her diligently. She liked that. They carried large, colourful pieces speculating on her love life, calling her the "Butterfly of Ballimaran". She was sporting. She offered them witty one-liners as repartee; counter-questioned upstart reporters; vexed them with detailed lectures on the intricacies of the khayal; and essentially entertained herself.

There was once a story about the wife of a city collector in north-west India having claimed that the *Begum* had put a hex on her "unsuspecting" husband and bewitched him to such an extent that he found every little pretext to run to Delhi. Begum Sahiba was enticing, large-hearted, free-spirited and loving. Men felt comfortable and strong in her presence, away from their manipulative, nagging wives; not attenuated at all. And, that was a heady feeling. She was also naughty and clever, and knew how to engage with society and with the media. She kept them hooked.

As I thought about the Begum's story, I wondered whether she had arrived at this set of "behaviours" after cool consideration or had she just gone with the flow in a natural, free-flowing manner without giving it any thought? Osho, the mystic, claims that women are, by nature, exhibitionists. He maintains that women love to show themselves off, and want men to look at them and adore and worship them. Men, on the other hand, (very conveniently) are voyeurs. They delight in spotting and "consuming" what they like.

But that wasn't the point. If a woman wanted complete adoration and surrender; if she wanted her lover to ravage her passionately one night but leave her alone the next; to respect her for her talent, and to also crave for her mind and companionship, would you say that she wanted too much? Moreover, which woman would, at least in conservative societies, openly declare that she needed sex frequently, on her terms, and with no strings attached? The Begum had made all this crystal clear.

Many Indian women would find it difficult to give straight answers to direct questions. But Begum Sahiba lived by her own convictions, and by being so open about them, had earned the respect and regard of the multitude that sought her audience. Now, she wanted me. It was obvious. But I couldn't belong to her or become just another conquest. I had to tell her that, and I used verse to convey my plight. She caught on, and responded to it with one of her own compositions…a *bandish.* We remained together all afternoon, all evening, all night. And then, I left.

I knew that I'd be back. I also knew that I could never poison my mind against her in spite of what lay ahead. There was merit in who she had become, how she operated and what she wanted from life. She was dedicated to her craft, and she had taken very generously to me. Her beliefs were entirely her own. No one needed to advise her or change her. Instead, I suspected that I would have to tweak some of my own opinions and prejudices.

With these and similar thoughts filling my mind, I stumbled out of her *haveli* into a dark, discreet night and meandered through the lanes of Chawri Bazar, sailing, drifting, and sometimes...floating.

****

I wish I Didn't "Knew"
In Defence of a Dying Language

I'd like to find out how an entire generation has gone from ..."I didn't know" to the now prevalent..."I *didint knew*"! A tidal wave of aspiration—the inpouring of people from the villages to the cities—and a mass churning of penny-*gyaan* (Learn English in three months!) has changed the language of the Brits for me, around me, and in most of my neighbourhoods. I feel sorely left out in the re-invented paradigm, and have no one to go to for help! Therefore, this attempt at self-counselling.

I'm from a simpler time when folk weren't overwhelmed by the knowledge-tsunami. There was neither an information-overload nor the pressure to be aware of everything all the time. It was alright to generally doodle; sit and stare, and watch life go by, one day at a time. One could opt to plunge into the fray, be competitive and pursue learning or choose to stay out of the race, be unreservedly at peace and still afford a decent lifestyle. (Or so, I believe. Smirking is allowed.)

In this monolithic dawn of cataclysmic proportions, however, I am beginning to feel decidedly out of depth. I am constantly bombarded by an emerging, new language that leaves me unsettled. I understand not one sacred word of it, and I'm yet to locate the resources to help me comprehend its structure. Let me explain. When I am sent text messages that say "*grt2meetu*" or when I am asked "*dint u knew her*" and when I'm told this by "*1ofmystudent*", please imagine my consternation for I do not know how to respond.

The "one of the many" but not in the plural, in particular, has me completely and utterly disoriented. I must avow that the number of occasions when I've wanted to throw the speaker (of such sentences) under a bus has been too many. Having to hear it not once, not twice, but a dozen times every twenty-four hours is far more disruptive than you can imagine. But I have not yet lost my sanity. I wish I could just cringe and run away each time I'm told by someone that X is "one of their best assignment". Or that Y is "one of the best film" that they have ever seen. Often I can't. Therefore, what I'm now doing is carrying the extra "Ss" in a soft hand bag, and just sliding them in quietly.

You might say that this is a rant in defence of an old language in a new environment. You might advise me to stop being judgmental, and start learning the "updated" version. You may say, "Be quick to change, ordinary mortal! Or, you'll be left behind!" You might also suspect that this is an insincere attempt at trying to figure out this modern parlance. You could accuse me of being overly dramatic. And, you may suggest that I am being anxious for no reason. An acquaintance called me yesterday, out of the blue, and asked, "*Didint you used to rode* Harley Davidsons?" I fell off my chair.

Who said I was distressed! I am solely trying to understand this phenomenon so that I can prepare myself for what the future might entail. You see, when I encounter people who ask me—"*Didint you went* to the party?" instead of the commonplace "Did you not go to the…?", I must confess that I am a tad flurried. I do not know whether it is permitted any more to say that I "couldn't go to the party" because what is more easily understood by my interlocutors today is the far more popular "I *could'nt went* to the party". I don't think I am ready yet to mouth the "I *didint went*" of my own accord. You can't force me!

Now perhaps you will comprehend the gravity of my situation. I must admit that the complete disowning of some grammatical terms from the erstwhile English has affected me and made me twitchy. "Wouldn't you, Couldn't you and Shouldn't you" have lost their place among the speakers here. Even more baffling is the fact that "haven't you had" has been totally extirpated from use. There isn't even a tomb in its memory. Instead, the "*Didint you had*" is applied with great alacrity. Most professionals use it today. Even (some) professors of the English language say it repeatedly. Therefore, it must be right! Or so the "*didint knews*" assume.

What do you mean "Give them hints." Wouldn't those be positively ignored? After all, who'd listen to someone using archaic terms such as "shall not" or, even worse… "shan't"! In a world dominated by technology, innovation, speed and creativity, who is to say that the need for language as it exists today will not be transformed in…say …a hundred years! Even this contemporary babble might have to alter itself.

Out of use and out of practice, several dialects and vernaculars have, in any case, vanished from the face of the earth. Several others are in dire need of resuscitation such as Aragonese, Avar, Cree, Manx, Tatar, Udmurt, Oromo and Quechua among others. Several others such as Magati Ke, spoken by the aboriginals of Australia, and Kallawaya, used in the Andes Mountains of Bolivia, or Tofa, spoken by the hunter gatherers of Central Siberia are already on the verge of extinction.

My entreaties about the convulsions in the English language are far more plebeian. I am aware that languages mutate with time. Spanglish and Hinglish are examples although they would qualify as hybrids. Even speech and interaction go through a metamorphosis. But the strangulation and asphyxiation of a language must surely classify as murder. And, the strange part is that no one really knows how and when this damage was done. *Did you think so that* a rot has set in? Or do you not think so? Having to respond to such questions is another one of my woes.

But I do have the energy to put the "think so that" into perspective. It is challenging to keep explaining this one. For example, Situation 1. A: Do you think we could get tickets for the Sufi music festival this month? B: Yes, I think so. Let me try. (There's a full stop after think so. Please!) C: Do you think we could afford a vacation this summer? D: Yes. I think so that we can. Beep! Beep! Beep! Beep! Beep! Beep! Beep! Beep! Beep! Beep! The clangour of the correction hammers is deafening in my mind, even as I recover from such affronts.

You might ask me whether the disfigurement of syntax and the deformation of grammar leave me sanguine. Ladies and Gentlemen! I assure you that I shall not agonize disproportionately over what happens. I am already in the throes of a catastrophe. Suffocated by the ironclad grip of clauses such as "*one of the many thing*" (not things) and the "*best of my friend*" (not friends, obviously), I might die a slow and painful death but I will not watch in horror the tragedy that has particularly struck the "more" and "most" series of words.

You must be apprised of the—*more greater*, *more bigger* and *more better*—sort of usages, if I can call them that. I wonder whether *more gooder* and *more badder* would actually make the import of these words that much *more grander*. If this is so much *more easier*, pray, why not the much *more difficulter*! Why become squeamish now? The British tried their best to destroy our textiles, our heritage and our culture, we are told. So, they truly deserve to have their language squarely and wholeheartedly wrecked and eradicated. More power to the demolition! It's only fair! Some of you must be *most happiest* doing this as it is the *most best* service you could do to your nation. Yikes!

I do accept that the process of using such a "parole" is democratic. It evolves on its own over time. I am also aware that communication and expression have to be comfortable, facile and smooth. They can't be coerced on speakers. There has to be flexibility and elasticity to a language, I say! Therefore, rules can be damned! And, non-converts can go to hell! And in spite of being frightfully enervated by this exercise, I am going to say something that I might regret.

I am going to request you (the ones who still speak the old language) with folded hands to acquaint yourself with this ground-breaking patter, argot, terminology… call it what you will! I was lagging behind pathetically and look where it has brought me! Implicitly addled and quite unhinged. That's how I feel. And this is what happens to those who are unwilling to change. So, be warned!

Forget the placement of the "the"s. Just put them anywhere! For example:- "Have you eaten *the* lunch? (It doesn't matter whose lunch. Just let it go!) Or, "Do you like listening to *the* music?" (Don't ask which music! Just grin and bear it!) Even worse will be "I'm *gonna* buy *the* new car during *the* Diwali or during vacations." (Their car! Their holidays. Let it be!) The last straw could be "After *the* Trump, Americans are *gonna* go running to *the* Canada." (That might happen! So, why complain?)

So, without further ado, and without making a federal case out of it, and of course, in the larger pursuit of learning something "new-born" and "far out", I hereby pledge my willingness to give this "language" a shot. So, help me God! In spite of the alarm bells going off in my head, in gazillions, actually, and despite every metal item around me rattling down the tin roof of my mind, and having fought Globus

Hysterícus, and still combating the gagging sensation in my throat and the feeling that something is blocking my airway, and struggling with the choking feeling in my neck and in my chest, I must profess that the English I have so far spoken…hasn't been compromised. It has merely been improvised. Amen!

****

No Bad Hair Days

You are what you eat, they say. That becomes so much more real after an encounter with breast cancer. So, after ten months of being on this radar, I have become …chia seeds, flax seeds, wheatgrass, beetroot, papayas, oranges, yoghurt and lemon juice. I have also become, in good measure, buttermilk, turmeric, apples, grapes and strawberries. But I must remember though that during the dreaded chemotherapy, they ask you to avoid berries because they could carry dirt or be contaminated. So, the one good shot you have at consuming something exotic like a blueberry or a raspberry goes for a toss. Instead, you find yourself swimming in lime and gooseberry juice and aloe vera and possibly an ocean full of coconut water. All super stuff, by the way. It depends on what your system can take.

Or, what it wants for it to be able to combat the scourge of the metallic taste the chemicals leave on the tongue.

This is what happened to me: After forty-eight years of being reasonably healthy, one fine evening (in retrospect, not so fine), I found a pea-sized lump just over my right breast. I acted with alacrity; immediately sharing the information with my spouse (whether or not he wanted to hear it); was warned against ignoring it or taking it lightly; and didn't do any such thing. You see...only two and a half months before the damn pea, my right knee had buckled suddenly during a promenade in the park. And that was just a month after I had put my entire weight into learning whatever little I did of the Salsa.

So, this is how I will retrace this journey. January 2016. Studying Spanish. Teaching French. Revising Urdu. Writing in English. Learning the guitar. All is well. Extremely fond of dancing. Can't resist the temptation any more. Therefore, Sunday classes. Twelve noon to 1.30 pm. Five...Six... Seven...Eight...Let's do the salsa! Bailando...Bailamos... Baile! For about a month. Good weather, too. The exams come up in February. Out goes the Salsa. Who wants to lag behind! Back to the Sedentary. Long hours at a study table, bent over reading material. Lots of writing practice, too. Walking a bit, off and on. And, that's when the knee buckled.

Done with the exams. Cleared the level. To be followed up by nearly forty-five days of long overdue renovation of the house—through most of March and much of April. (Hadn't happened for ten years because I wasn't home to watch over it. The hubby is a pilot. Can't be in station (Delhi) for too long. Here comes the camel under the mountain (kindly go back to the Hindi for the meaning of that sentence)! Watching over the reconstruction of the house. Picked up this collection of short stories. Writing fresh pieces. Editing the old ones. Not moving much. Smoking like a chimney. The body; the cells—who knows what else happens inside that huge machine in there. Every little bit must have been so very baffled. From hyper to still. And from still to completely stagnant. The cells protest. Wham! Out comes the cancer! But there's yet another interlude before the big bang.

Spanish Next Level. B 2. The last level. The toughest level begins. It has four sub levels. This is B 2.1. Wonderful professor. Great material to study. Topography. Food. Culture. The entire Latin American repertoire out there to explore. How thrilling! Dazzling! Challenging! June. The exams come up again. Marking will be pretty strict this time. Studying, as usual. But there's a sense that the concentration is at 99.99 only. There's that gap. Hasn't happened in the past. This collection goes to the back burner. A plan to visit Europe has come through in May (after three years of no holidays) for the husband. The idea is to visit Vienna, Budapest, Salzburg and Prague. The lands of Gustav Klimt; Franz Liszt; Wolfgang Amadeus Mozart and Franz Kafka in that order. Too exciting for words!

Must go to the Musikverein. Have to see the Klimt museum. Shall look for Beethoven's house in Vienna. Have to try the Wiener Schnitzel. Will thoroughly enjoy the Schonbrunn Palace. A cruise down the Danube in Budapest is a done thing. Shall dunk into a thermal bath there. Will walk across the Chain Bridge. Try their wine? But...of course! Strauss, Haydn, Mahler and Mozart in Salzburg, without a doubt. With some luck, will buy CDs. Vinyl should be better. The Viennese Waltz, The London Symphonies, The Trumpet Concerto, The Resurrection, The Marriage of Figaro, Moonlight Sonata...the list is endless.

Anyway, much is happening inside the head. There are the exams to handle. Stories to tell. A film to make. So much ambition! And now, there's a bloody lump. June 15. Oh...I forgot to mention that in between all this, the teeth cave in, and there's a root canal episode. I should've known right when the knee buckled (for the first time in my life) that 2016 was going to be my "over-hauling" year. Anything that could be repaired came up for repair. Even the knee got a bit of a boost—some stem cells business. But this is the BC story. So, I'll stick to that.

So, where was I? The notorious Breast C. They also have the temerity to call it benign, kind and innocent. Clang! Clang! Clang! Perhaps it is. Who knows? Compared to all the other bloodcurdling Cs, perhaps it is! Anyway, I take a Spanish exam one morning, and go straight into a mammography. The clock's ticking. Less than forty-eight hours to go on that trip. Tick! Tock! Tick! "It's not looking very good," says the technician. "But we'll know for sure after the ultrasound." Big relief? Ditto…during the ultrasonography. "I can't say for sure that it's looking good. When did you last have an ultrasound?" I look up at the ceiling. I cannot recall. Perhaps it was ten years ago. Not sure. Now, this is where one errs. Please have your health regularly checked up! The most atrocious things can just… pop up.

Reports. Gynaecologist. Surgeon. The running around happens. There is a reasonable amount of panic but both my husband and I are stoic. "We'll take it as it comes." The surgeon does a physical examination. Suggests a biopsy. A close friend is a doctor in a rival hospital. I don't tell her anything. Not yet. Why bother her! She must be busy packing, too. We are flying off the next morning. The result of the biopsy will be out only in forty-eight hours. I am loathe to even consider cancelling my trip. I am going. So, we end up in Vienna. June 19. It is beautiful. Clean and peaceful and artistic. There's a deluge of Klimt's 'The Kiss'. It has been successfully commercialized. It's on umbrellas and bags and sunglass covers and on coasters and mugs and anything else than you can imagine. On the other hand, his Judith and Adele and Hope are available to only those who seek them.

My nineteen-year-old son, also an art aficionado, is with me as we take in the paintings. We take a coffee break and talk about them. The others in our group, ten of them, are pursuing their own interests. We will soon re-group for a visit to the Schonbrunn Palace (I later find out that it has 1441 rooms). I am looking forward to hearing all about Maria Theresa—the only female ruler of the Habsburg Empire. We are shown, among many different ornate rooms, her daughter Marie Antoinette's room. Napoleon stayed here, as well. The magnificent gardens boast of Neptune's Fountain, a facsimile of the one in Florence, Italy. The story of the mythical Greek sea goddess Thetis and her son, Achilles is touching. Remember the heel? It wasn't dipped in and remained vulnerable.

Tonight, June 20, my world will fall apart (for a while) but I don't know that yet. I do remember, though, that my best friend will collect the biopsy report in Delhi and send me a succinct message in Vienna. At the end of a long day, when we return to our chambers, my husband goes on to join his buddies in their room for a drink. I stay back and access the WiFi. There, in the inbox, is that earth-shattering line—"Surgery might be imminent. But a decision can be taken when you return." I do the first thing that I normally do (or did) in a crisis—pick up a cigarette and stay calm. I do hope to continue to keep my wits about me at all times... but... smoking...I've had to give up almost entirely. I cheat in my mind and sometimes find myself taking a puff or two in my dreams even today. But the pleasure of lighting up is more or less just a pipedream now. (Pun intended.) And since I don't drink (except the occasional wine or beer), I find myself currently without vice! How boring!

To return to my buddy, Sangita, on that night, I find her standing alone outside a hotel in beautiful Wien, smoking, and asking herself, "How do you want to deal with this? Do you want to panic? Or, do you want to be brave?" There's only one answer to such a question. I stub out the stick and go back to my room. There, I take some deep breaths, make adjustments to my face, put my chin up and walk over to where the gang is holed. Would I like a drink? Will it be a beer? I don't remember what I said. But I had a reasonable amount of grit that night. I stayed cool and didn't mention a word of it to anyone, the spouse included. Why rain on his parade! That night as we slept, I thought of a giant taking away my breast; having carved it out with a knife, and leaving one ginormous hole in my chest. So, I turned the other way, fell off the grid, and rested in the arms of Morpheus.

We were to leave for Budapest soon. I had my mask on, I think. Even I couldn't have made out…that I was worried! First class on the Euro Rail is excellent. There's a lovely countryside to feast my eyes upon. Large, grey windmills with red and white tips like propellers of an aircraft. Cottages dotting the landscape. Hmm… We reach the Hungarian capital, check in quickly into a hotel on the Pest side, and go over to Buda right away. But before that, while waiting for the others to arrive, and seated under the shade of a horse chestnut tree outside the hotel, I tell my better half the truth. "Looks like it might happen," I say. "How do you feel about it?" he asks, keeping his equilibrium. "I'll be okay," I respond. We smile faintly. We shall be in it together. But most of all, we'll be strong. That's it! We take a funicular and go up Castle Hill to see the History Museum and to take in a majestic view of the city from that height. It's a view that one shall never forget.

Through the 24th of June to the 26th, we visit Salzburg where a visit to Mozart's house happens. Its façade is yellow, reminding me of Van Gogh and of madness and of anguish and of the lump. There's also a trip to see the Salt mines at Berchtesgaden (a municipality in the German Bavarian Alps) and to Werfen in Salzburg to see the Eisriesenwelt ice caves, the largest ice caves in the world. I put my repaired knee to test as we have to first climb and then descend 700 steps over and above a one hour trek to the cave's entrance. The knees manage. And will act up towards the end of the trip. But for now, there's Hitler's summer residence, his sister's home in Obersalzburg. And the Hohenwerfen Castle where the film *Where Eagles Dare* was filmed. There's also the much-mentioned fact that *The Sound of Music* was filmed in Salzburg. Its songs are run on a loop in the bus until we request for them to be stopped. Twice is enough. Instead, we are introduced to Giuseppe Verdi, the Italian opera composer. Quite a change!

The doctor friend, who will later become my guardian during chemo and radiation, has a hunch that something is amiss. She asks me whether I'm ok. I lie. I tell her that I'm just tired. A visit to the Swarovski showroom at Innsbruck which lies halfway between Munich (Germany) and Verona (Italy) in western Austria and which has hosted the 1964 and 1976 winter Olympics is supercalifragilisticexpialidocious. We shall soon take a train to Linz and from there, another one to Praha. When we enter the Century Hotel in Prague,

I notice photographs of Kafka in the lobby. I ask questions and am told that the tormented novelist worked in Room 214 of this (the old Insurance Building) structure from 1908 to 1922. How serendipitous! To find oneself literally walking the path that he did! I also thought of his troubled relationship with his father and of the death of his sisters and of all the demons in his head. Tragedy and creativity must be related.

Walking through the narrow cobbled streets of Prague, we reach the Old Town Square to see the astronomical clock. From the corner of his eye, my son notices an Andy Warhol exhibition. He has to see it. So, we do. The familiar Marilyn Monroes and the quirky Soup Can series. An absolute treat! Must I tell him that I might have to go under the scalpel very soon? I don't. Soon, we will take a train for Dresden, and then another one to Leipzig and a third to Frankfurt before returning home where I will have to visit the doctor and hear the naked truth with my own ears. I will have to sacrifice my breast and there will be trauma. But nothing prepares me for what he tells us. "You'll have surgery on the 4th of July. We'll remove the lymph nodes. You'll have reconstruction the same day. Be prepared for a six to eight month journey from thereon." Eight months? I scream. What about my Spanish exams? And my students at the French? What do you mean?

"You'll have to make some changes," he says, calmly. And suggests that I meet the plastic surgeon instead. She's a petite, boyish, no nonsense doctor. Very straightforward. "We'll take these muscles from the abdomen and create something organic for you, if that's what you want," she says. I nod. I don't like the idea of carrying around prosthetics (even figuratively). Have you stopped smoking yet? she asks me. So, I light up for the last time around midnight on the 3rd of July. I'm supposed to be fasting in anticipation of all that wear and tear the next morning. My partner keeps his shirt On. I remain completely silent. I haven't contacted anyone. Not even my family. My son is told about it, and he's equally resilient. "What would you like me to do?" is all he asks. I don't know how he coped with all this. I do not even want to ask him. He'll have to relive the pain. To think that his mother might just die must've been difficult for him. But he's a musician, and that must have helped.

So, while America is set to celebrate its Independence Day, anesthesia is induced upon me. Several hours later, when I'm wheeled out and brought to a room, my husband, my son, my brother, who has rushed from Jaipur, and my dearest friend—four of the five great men in my life—my father has passed away—are there to receive me. I have pipes coming out of my body. I am completely bandaged up and a little bent. But I have surprisingly not lost my sense of humour. I crack jokes and even have a picture taken, all contorted. My brother does that to me—lifts my spirits up. My son brings his books and spends time looking after me. I am extremely touched. My friend finishes a full day at work and then comes over to stay. I can never thank him enough. My husband is a tower of strength, supervising everything at the hospital and also flying for his airline, whenever duty calls. He's amazing!

The next four days in the hospital are spent coming to terms with the surroundings and dealing with the changes on the body. The doctors are satisfied with the progress. The surgeon (who removed the tissue) is so kicked about his handiwork that he wants to take a picture of the "new material" for "medical reasons". I joke with him about not promoting it on Twitter. He doesn't get it. I am discharged and am back home, taking the fifty stairs uphill, slowly but surely. I pack a bag with my books and such and am dropped at my mum-in-law's place. My husband has a flight and won't be in town over the next four days. I still haven't told my doctor friend about my situation. And to make matters even more interesting, my phone conks off, thus shutting me out from the world and giving me my needed peace and quiet. I had been reading Milan Kundera throughout the trip and had then moved to an Orhan Pamuk, and on to the brilliant 'The Elephant Vanishes' by Haruki Murakami.

There's also Neruda and Borges and Garcia Lorca. I read with unquenchable thirst. I cannot do anything else during those first few days.

A week down the line, when I come back to my own house, I know that I must call 'her'. She deserves to know. She's on rounds when she takes my call. "Where have you been? What happened to your phone? Why was it switched off? Are you alright?" She has questions. I request her to sit down for what I am about to tell her. She is shocked, a little upset, but mostly taken aback. She informs the rest of the gang. Meanwhile, I have told my sister about it and my other friends...very carefully. Walking on eggshells. Some of my (so called) friends (and I don't know the art of making many) are completely shocked but don't come rushing over. Why would they? I am not the sticky kind either. I tell them that I am absolutely fine and that there is no cause for concern. Yet others, some of who—I've known only over the last couple of years, are by my side in no time.

One doesn't know how people will react. I've never really given it much thought. But it was interesting to observe how they tried to make themselves useful when confronted with such information. "It's as common as a common cold. Nothing to worry about," said one friend. "Why don't ...You... give it a go", I felt like telling her, if it is that simple. But I don't. I'll have to repeatedly give up rage, resentment and anger, whenever they come back and bite me. I let everything pass, just putting the words in the archives for use such as this one. Another hears about it and starts remembering all the people in her family who have had some sort of cancer or the other. Well! What do you say to that? A third starts telling me about the pain that she is going through because both her sons have gone off to college. A fourth has just returned from a trip to the Greek island, Crete. She goes: "This is what happens when you smoke." And then spends the next twenty minutes being spiteful about her sister-in-law who travelled with her. A fifth has called to get some clarity on media studies. Her son is poised to enter college. All she wants to find out is "right breast or left?"

Some of my male friends are bewildered. It's also got to do with the "boob", I reckon. They don't know what to do with the information other than mumble, "Are you alright now?" I'll take that. I'm better now, I tell them. During this time, I get to read books that have been on the shelf for twenty years, waiting patiently. There's no guilt this time about putting up my feet and being at it all day. There are regular visits to the hospital to see if the stitches are healing. The skin is so tight that I can neither feel it nor be comfortable in it. My stomach is as taut as a Bharatanatyam dancer's but looks and feels like tanned leather.

I am asked to take it easy—not to drive; not to take the stairs; not to lift weights etc. I have no idea why I don't listen; not entirely. I do all of the above with the result that I have to be re-stitched—the abdomen bit, that is. Let's just leave this story at that. I'll tell you more if you ask me privately. Meanwhile, the most delightful thing happens to me. I am completely overwhelmed. A dozen women (from my life) have come together in various groups to become my support system over the next six months. (And I've not even put in the effort to make friends.) My best friend, Kanwaldeep, is a blessing. He checks on me each and every day, and has compassion, generosity and abundant patience throughout the journey.

These men and women will feed me; take me on trips; come home for conversations; two will teach me how to make soup; some will dance with me when I recover; they will rush to my aid when I need it; they'll fuss over me; and tell me over and over again that I am doing brilliantly. They will laugh at my jokes and put up with my constant ribbing of them. With a bald pate or with a turban around it, they will tell me that I look absolutely regal. No bad hair days! The comb's in cold storage. And that is yet another story I must tell you. The doctor (guardian angel) takes all my records from the one hospital and shifts them to her side of the city.

She then consults with her friends and fixes up a meeting with an oncologist. He turns out to be a sensitive man with eyes that twinkle, who tells me with great care that chemotherapy affects each person differently. That it is about the strength of the mind and about the personality. He says he knows that I'll do well. And, I do. Throughout the thirteen cycles that I am given, I am mostly alright. There is a point when I'm hailing cabs at 8 am and going for chemo, all by myself. Why take up anyone's time? What I do endure, however, is a bitter taste on my tongue, some heaviness in the head, a very sore throat and a general feeling of being tentative; not fully okay but not severely ill either. But I show pluck. People who bump into me here and there are completely unaware that I am "ill". It doesn't show. I smile a lot and continue to use wit. My students are back and I teach them happily. I read and write whenever my eyes support me. And, I keep at my guitar classes. My instructor is thrilled. He brings me flowers. "This is to celebrate your spirit," he says.

To tell you a little more about chemotherapy, I had a chemo port installed under my skin on my chest on the left side. This then helped me take the poke of the injection better each time I went for the procedure. So, instead of having a needle stuck into my veins for five hours each week (and this, over and above the weekly blood tests and injections to keep the blood count up), I had the one prick when the needle went into the chemo port and then, just fell into a semi-conscious slumber while the medicines went into the body. Max Hospital has a swanky set up dedicated purely to chemotherapy in Lajpat Nagar in south Delhi. A sort of five-star day care resort—neat and tidy and calm. (The people who come in mess up the loos. But then that is a reflection on our hygiene and our habits, and we should start paying more attention to decency as Indians.) One just walks into this centre, pays up, and lets the people there take over.

Day One, they made me stand at the billing counter for quite a while. When they wanted feedback, I gave it to them unabashedly. After that day, I walked straight into a small glass cabin with a recliner and a television to catch the news, with a full glass window, with a view of the sky and of the birds therein, and of plants and trees, and sat there quietly. No concrete towers blocked my view. And I did not have to hang by at the cash counter. Someone from the other side came to me and collected the money. There in that serene room, while undergoing chemotherapy, I have had the pleasure of listening to my friend run an Osho discourse for me. I have also enjoyed the Qawwalis of the Sabri Brothers that my husband has played for my benefit. I have been able to eat and drink while the medicines have gone into me! And I have narrated one of my short stories to a very cheerful oncologist in charge who would come regularly to check on me.

And just before chemotherapy began in end August, I had my Art on by going to Rome to see the Sistine Chapel. I told my oncologist that I would be happier and therefore stronger if I could just gaze at the Chapel ceiling and at the Last Judgment and come back with some books. He smiled and let me go. So, I went. I got to see Michelangelo's David, too, in Florence, where I also got to buy a print of Klimt's Kiss, which hangs in my bedroom today. I also saw the magnificence of Neptune's Fountain. Visits to the Trevi Fountain in Roma, the Pantheon, the Colosseum, the Piazza Navona, Capitol Hill, the Spanish Steps, the Fountain of Four Rivers, the Fontana della Barcaccia and the Vatican Museum were all fruitful and invigorating for they prepared me for the next six-eight months of chemo and radiation.

That is the other thing—Do know yourself and find out what works for you! I must admit that I was quite anxious about what the chemo will do to me. So, a friend very kindly helped me contact another friend whose spouse had been through it. Talking to her helped put things in perspective. I must confess that, contrary to what is expected, I did not read a single word on the subject so as to keep myself uncluttered and un-opinionated. I remember even singing during chemo. And, eating whatever I craved for.

A friend, Soniya, very kindly invited me over to her place several times after chemo. So, there was sambar dosa and there was choley bhaturey and samosas and Chinese food. I realized that whatever makes you happy will keep you happy while you handle your travails. Each time I felt I was going mad, I picked up my Art Books and was transported to a world where one does not complain. So, my complete gratitude to all the great artists, painters, sculptors and poets of the world for they protected me from my own pain and delivered me from my distress.

****

Making the Cancer Journey Easier

- After mastectomy, reconstruction is possible (with organic material as in your own muscle instead of a prosthetic) but that leads to severe stretching of the skin, which is uncomfortable but that gets better with time (say, in about six months).
- Two weeks into chemo, the hair starts falling off. Just shave it at one go; order a wig in advance, wrap around your scarves in fun ways. Be liberated! The eyebrows become faint. Nothing too scary. Just different.
- Chemo may make one nauseous or constipated. There are homoeopathic medicines to counter these things. They can be tried.
- Fortify and build immunity before chemo starts

by consuming a lot of wheatgrass and gooseberry and beetroot and carrot juice.

- Fruits become great friends. Lots of fluids must be consumed. Eating whatever suits one keeps the morale up. (I almost completely gave up meats. Just didn't feel like having them. I also went easy on oily and fried food. But if I felt like having a poori one day, I just had it.)
- Keep walking and breathing deep; watch films; meet people; do whatever it is that you normally do. Being reasonably active is healthier. I continued with work and with my hobbies, tapering off just after my chemotherapy ended.The cumulative effect, they called it. Fatigue and joint pains. But during the four months of chemo, I was more or less okay. I even travelled.
- Never lose an opportunity to have fun. Laugh whenever you can. It is not the end of the world. I remember dancing my heart out on my 49th birthday in November 2016 at the peak of my chemo; three months into it. Chemotherapy is tough but it can be endured. Worse could've happened. Remember that.
- Radiation is much simpler. It just chars the skin and plays havoc with the throat, making

swallowing difficult for a while but the process itself is completely painless. The procedure takes time. There's too much waiting involved, and there's the to and fro to the hospital. But other than that, it is light on you.

- Keep your family close by. They go through worse if they find out that they cannot help alleviate your pain. Keep talking to them. Tell them what you want.
- A creative outlet can be a boon, as has been the process of writing this piece, for me. So, I thank you for being here. If you've enjoyed this, do arm others who might be going through what I did, with this information. It might help.
- Finally, there's nothing like a little humour to handle just about anything. I'm still making the effort to deal with the after effects of my story. Let's hope I make it. Meanwhile, Good Luck To You! Fare thee well! And, Take Care!

****

You…are eternally pure consciousness…the Witness;
in need of nothing! So, live happily!

—Ashtavakra Gita (Chapter 15)